Staff

Founder and Executive Editor Meredith Allard

Deputy Editor Susan Arenstein

Senior Editor Paula Day

Contributors

Lynn Aprill
Joel Brickell
J. Thomas Brown
Bethan Charles
Lisa Gordon
Wendy Howe
Benjamin Hulme
Nancy Lee
Kim McCollum
Shannon Monroe
J.P. O'Connell
Jenny Quinlan
Billie Holladay Skelley
L.E. Smith
Amadea Tanner
Rachel Thompson
Salinda Tyson

EDITORIAL OFFICE

2654 W. Horizon Ridge Pkwy
Suite B5-364
Henderson, NV 89052

For advertising, contact:
copperfieldreview@gmail.com

For submission guidelines:
www.copperfieldreviewquarterly.com

ISSN: 1533-3736

Cover Photo Credit:
J. Lee

www.copperfieldreviewquarterly.com
www.copperfieldreview.com.
Copperfield Press

SPRING 2022

COPPERFIELD REVIEW QUARTERLY

A Journal for Readers and Writers
of Historical Fiction

CONTENTS

OUR CONTRIBUTORS

Award-winning poet and educator **Lynn Aprill** has published work recently in *Bramble, Willows Wept Review, Quartet*, and others. *Channeling Matriarchs*, her first chapbook with Finishing Line Press, was released in August 2021. She resides with her husband and various dogs on 40 acres in Northeast Wisconsin. Her work can be found at https://lynnaprill.weebly.com/

Joel Brickell is a Soto Zen practitioner living in Dallas Texas and writes poetry "to stay awake to the present moment and the sufferings of others." His poems have appeared in Frogpond and Modern Haiku.

J. Thomas Brown lives in Richmond, Virginia with his wife and family. His short stories and poems have appeared in numerous magazines and anthologies. Other published works include two historical fiction novels, a patremoir, and a short story collection.

Lisa Gordon's fiction has been published in *Paper Darts, Storychord, Hypertext*, and others. She is working on a novel about Cornelius Garland, a Black physician from Alabama who founded and operated the first and only Black hospital in Boston, from 1908-1928.

Wendy Howe is an English teacher and freelance writer who lives in Southern California. Her poetry reflects her interest in myth, diverse landscapes, and ancient cultures. Over the years, she has been published in an assortment of journals both online and in print. Among them: *The Poetry Salzburg Review, The Interpreter's House, Stirring A Literary Collection, Eye To The Telescope, Yellow Medicine Review, The Orchards Journal, The Tower Journal, Word Gathering Press*, and several anthologies,. Most recently, her work appeared in a poetic anthology celebrating the work and legacy of Ursula K. Le Guin.

Benjamin Hulme is a post-graduate from the University of Aberystwyth, Wales, who spends the majority of his spare time, when not with friends, writing. It was due to a lecturer at his university, during a scriptwriting seminar who asked if he had ever considered writing a novel or fiction. From there he learned all he could and is still learning, and with his particular love of history, it is only natural that most of his stories tend to be set in a historical setting. He is a keen enthusiast for reading and learning, always open to new experiences and travel.

Richard Koman has been an attorney, a technology reporter, book editor, and led a nonprofit project to distribute free books to schools, the Uganda Digital Bookmobile.

Nancy Lee is a wife, mother, and poet living in Bar Harbor, Maine.

Kim McCollum lives in Bozeman, MT with her blended menagerie of 5 kids and 3 dogs. Her home is full of love but rarely tidy. She is a graduate of Barnard College and is currently pursuing her MLA in Creative Writing from Harvard University. Her work has appeared in *The Dillydoun Review* and *Fiction on the Web*. She was a finalist in Now Novel's Character Writing Contest. She is the author of the travel blog happygoluckytraveler.com. In her spare time, Kim loves to ski, hike, travel, and drink wine.

Shannon Monroe is a doctoral candidate at the Institute for the Study of the Ancient World (NYU), where she researches Central Asian history through bioarchaeological investigations. She lives in Connecticut with her husband and two children.

J. P. O'Connell has worked as an editor and writer for a variety of newspapers and magazines including *Time Out, The Guardian, The Times*, and *The Daily Telegraph*. J. P. has also written several books, including a novel, a celebration of letter-writing, a spice encyclopedia, and, most recently, an analysis of David Bowie's favorite books and the ways they influenced his music. J. P. lives in London.

Jenny Quinlan, aka Jenny Q, is an editor and cover designer specializing in historical fiction. As founder of Historical Editorial, she has helped hundreds of authors achieve their publishing goals. She also serves as chair of the Historical Novel Society North America Conference. Jenny lives on a farm in Virginia with her family and a spoiled-rotten German Shepherd.

Billie Holladay Skelley received her Bachelor's and Master's degrees from the University of Wisconsin-Madison. Billie has written several health-related articles for both professional and lay journals. She has been published in journals and books such as the *American Journal of Nursing* and *Chicken Soup for the Soul*. An award-winning author, she also has written eleven books for children and teens, including *Eagle the Legal Beagle, Ollie the Autism-Support Collie*, and *Weaver the Diabetic-Alert Retriever*.

L.E. Smith has two novels of historical fiction published (one about churches burned deliberately in 1970s Burlington, VT/another about the murder of John Lennon). Smith has a third novel published and a book of short stories, some of those published separately in university lit mags.

Amadea Tanner is a writer and filmmaker born and raised in Los Angeles, but currently based in Baltimore. A graduate of Chapman University with bohemian degrees in screenwriting and French, she is partial to witty banter, philosophical musing, and toeing the line between drama and comedy. This story is her literary debut, originally published on the site Jerry Jazz Musician. You can find her in the ether @amadea_cadence.

Rachel Thompson is an author, editor, writing coach, and a former Managing Editor with *Room*, where she remains on the editorial collective. She's the host of the Write, Publish, and Shine Podcast. Find out more about her and sign up for her Writerly Love Letters at rachelthompson.co.

Salinda Tyson has lived a long time in Northern California and now lives in North Carolina, but misses earthquakes and ocean fog.

DEAR READERS

Our deepest fear is not that we are inadequate. Our deepest fear is that we are powerful beyond measure. It is our light, not our darkness that most frightens us. We ask ourselves, Who am I to be brilliant, gorgeous, talented, fabulous? Actually, who are you not to be? You are a child of God. Your playing small does not serve the world. There is nothing enlightened about shrinking so that other people won't feel insecure around you. We are all meant to shine, as children do. We were born to make manifest the glory of God that is within us. It's not just in some of us; it's in everyone. And as we let our own light shine, we unconsciously give other people permission to do the same. As we are liberated from our own fear, our presence automatically liberates others.
                    ~Marianne Williamson

For me, spring brings wildflowers that bloom briefly before the desert sun gets too hot. The yellow, purple, and pink flowers everywhere I look are reminders to enjoy these rare Las Vegas moments when the weather is just right. For me, spring means baseball—Los Angeles Dodgers baseball, specifically. If you're a fan of a different team, that's all right. I still like you.

I've been thinking a lot lately about the above quote from Marianne Williamson. I've read *A Return to Love*, the book from which the quote comes, but recently I realized that the quote spoke directly to the part in me that has been struggling the most lately—the part that feels like it needs to dim the light I have been striving for years to ignite. Williamson says, "Your playing small does not serve the world. There is nothing enlightened about shrinking so that other people won't feel insecure around you." Suddenly, I realized that I've been playing small to make those around me feel better. Perhaps you have too.

A few years ago a friend at work was so happy for me when a local magazine featured an article about *The Copperfield Review* that she posted a link to the article on our school's message board. As soon as I saw her post, I thought, "Oh no. This isn't going to be good."

I learned a long time ago that people aren't always happy when good things happen to someone else. When I was living in California, an article about my writing and publishing appeared in *The Los Angeles Times* and I told a few teachers I worked with about it. I thought it was cool, that's all.

The next day I heard from a friend that the talk in the staff room was about me: "She thinks she's so special now?" I shuddered at the knowledge that people were speaking negatively about me, especially over something I meant to be positive. That's when I slipped the dimmer over my light and stopped sharing anything about my writing or publishing with anyone.

Photo credit: Joel Holland

Over the years, the story never changed. I published a few successful novels and lost some friends. I finished my Ph.D. and lost some friends. Upon my return to teaching, we were asked what we did over summer vacation. I told the truth—I worked on my novel and created CRQ, a print edition of a literary journal I began 20 years ago. If the administrator had rolled her eyes any further back she would have spent the rest of her life staring at her own brain. What was so terrible about my response? I didn't spend my summer traveling, which was the most common answer. I was writing and editing. I wasn't bragging. She asked and I answered.

Suddenly, I began slinking around, my head hung low, avoiding eye contact with anyone. I was embarrassed (again).

Finally, it occurred to me (I'm a little slow sometimes)—why am I the one hiding? What have I done wrong? Does the fact that I've stayed stubbornly true to my dreams mean I have to feel embarrassed about it for the rest of my life? Why do I feel the need to explain away my successes when I don't expect anyone else to explain away theirs?

I had been letting others make me feel small, but that's my fault, not theirs. People can have whatever reactions they want. It's up to me to remember to, as Marianne Williamson says, "make manifest the glory of God that is within us."

When I'm writing, or when I'm editing CRQ, I'm manifesting the glory of God that is within me. If you're not a religious person, that's okay. You can think of it as the universe, or life, or Uncle Bob. It doesn't matter what you call it as long as you realize, like Dorothy in *The Wizard of Oz*, that you already have the power. No apologies required.

I've decided that I will no longer hide from my successes. I've earned every single one with years of hard work. Whenever I'm tempted to cower from acknowledgment of that hard work, I'll remember Williamson's words: "And as we let our own light shine, we unconsciously give other people permission to do the same. As we are liberated from our own fear, our presence automatically liberates others."

Amen.

Sending you best wishes and the courage to let your own light shine, whatever your light is, wherever you are on your journey.

See you in July.

Meredith

Meredith Allard, Executive Editor
Copperfield Review Quarterly

WANT TO MAKE A GREAT FIRST IMPRESSION?

FIVE TIPS FOR DESIGNING A HISTORICAL FICTION COVER

By Jenny Quinlan

I should preface this wonderful article by Jenny with the disclosure that she is my cover designer and I think her work is amazing. She created the gorgeous cover for *The Duchess of Idaho* and she also created the two *Hembry Castle* covers. Although Jenny isn't accepting new book cover clients, she has some words of wisdom to share about how to make sure your historical novel cover stands out from the crowd.

* * * * *

You've written a book and it's about to be published! Congratulations!

If you have a traditional publisher, you may not have much input on your cover. Traditional publishers rely on their marketing departments to determine how to position your book in the marketplace, and that includes cover art. If you're self-publishing, you have complete creative control over your cover, and if your cover isn't selling your book as you'd hoped, you have the ability to redo your cover and breathe some new life into your sales.

Whichever path to publication you are taking, it helps to study the marketplace and keep these tips in mind when it comes to choosing your book's cover.

1) Remember that the purpose of your book cover is to sell your book.

Too many authors lose sight of this goal, particularly with their first book. It's easy to get wrapped up in the idea that all of your main characters need to be portrayed or a certain theme has to come forth or a pivotal scene needs to be depicted. But the only job your cover has is to sell your book. And to be able to do this successfully, you have to put your attachment to the story aside and look at it from the eyes of the consumer. What type of reader is most likely to buy your book? (And don't say all of them! Identify your target audience.) What do they expect to see on the cover of a book they're thinking about buying? What do bestselling covers in your genre look like? And if you're hiring a professional, listen to their advice. A good designer knows what a good cover in your genre looks like.

2) A sense of time and place is important. And so is historical accuracy.

We all know that women (and sometimes men) in period clothing on historical covers has been a trend for many years. That's because clothing is the quickest way to convey the time period in which a story takes place when it comes to historicals. But it better be the right clothing. If you put a Tudor gown on a medieval cover, readers will notice. And call it out for all to see. The same goes for another popular trend, using a setting to convey time and place. If you're using a cityscape that features a prominent building that wasn't there during the time your story takes place, readers will notice. And call it out for all to see. So, just like in your story, it's important to get the historical details right. But what if you don't want a character on your cover? Trends exist to help here too. Old houses, old streets, symbols, maps, and paintings of battles and historical events can all be found on historical fiction covers. Font can also be used to evoke a sense of the past. Just be sure you choose a font that is clearly legible.

3) Paying attention to trends is also important.

Trends exist for a reason: they sell books. There's a reason why the big four have big marketing departments to identify target markets and the elements of covers that sell books. Put their marketing departments to work for you too! If your cover is too different from what readers are used to seeing, odds are good that they'll skip right over it. Pay attention to trends coming from the big houses. Everything from composition elements, model placement, fonts, colors, and keywords in titles. Headless women, characters shown from the back, and "split screen" covers with a character up top and a setting below have all been popular trends. Illustrated covers are starting to pop up with more regularity, as are bold primary colors with big fonts. When you start to see similar covers coming from the big four, pay attention. Their readers are your readers too, so give your book a cover that can compete with them.

4) Less is more.

Your cover should evoke a sense of the story and not necessarily be a literal interpretation. Resist the urge to clutter the cover with too many elements. Resist the urge to recreate a specific scene down to the last detail. Chances are your designer can't do that anyway, and the scene has no meaning for a reader who hasn't yet read the book. You want to catch the eye with an impactful image and text that's easy to read.

5) Your title and blurb are only slightly less important than your cover.

Together your cover, your title, and your back cover blurb create the foundation for your book's success. Your cover catches their eye, your title makes them curious, and your blurb seals the deal. Don't skimp on these other elements. Once again, study trends. Look to keywords. Look to length and rhythm of titles. Look to what is selling and read their blurbs. Most follow a fairly similar formula. Yours should too. If your blurb is too short, you won't engage readers. If it's too long, you risk giving so much away that they don't feel the need to read the book. Give your book the best chance at success by devoting time to strategically crafting these elements.

"MANY STORIES MATTER. STORIES HAVE BEEN USED TO DISPOSSESS AND TO MALIGN. BUT STORIES CAN ALSO BE USED TO EMPOWER, AND TO HUMANIZE. STORIES CAN BREAK THE DIGNITY OF A PEOPLE. BUT STORIES CAN ALSO REPAIR THAT BROKEN DIGNITY."

~ CHIMAMANDA NGOZI ADICHIE

Everyone has a story.
What's yours?

WHY WE NEED TO
SHARE OUR STORIES

By Nancy Lee

Two things I've learned in my 42 years are that, first, we never know what life has in store for us, and two, we are not alone.

Five years ago my son was diagnosed with autism. My husband and I were at our wit's end. We knew next to nothing about autism and we had to learn quickly. While my husband and I had each other, we still felt isolated, alone. We didn't know anyone else in our situation and we thought we were on our own.

Of course, we did our research. We learned. Then, encouraged by my husband, I began to write about my experiences. I began to tell our story as parents of an autistic child. I shared our ups and our downs. I shared our triumphs and our challenges. I was raw and honest, and soon other parents of autistic children responded. They shared their stories, and I was amazed to discover that they were experiencing many of the same joys and difficulties as I was. My husband and I weren't alone after all. There were others out there who understood us. What a revelation that was.

We've all heard the saying, "Everyone has a story." And it's true. We all have life experiences, good and bad, and there are times when we're certain that we're the only ones in the world who have ever had our troubles. No one else understands. Sometimes, we get so caught up in our own worries that we forget that everyone around us has their worries too. We think we're all alone and we keep our stories hidden in the dark as though our stories are something we should be ashamed of when they're not. Our lives are like quilts, stitched together in patchwork style, but the thing we learn when we share our stories is that people share more of those patches than we realize. People share a lot in our common humanity, and sharing our stories helps us to recognize that in a more visceral way.

If you're willing, if you're brave enough, you can share your story. You can tell others your truth. You don't have to shout it from the highest mountaintop. Look around you. See what support groups are available, online or in-person. Find professional help. Talk to those closest to you. Write something for your local paper or on your own blog. You might be surprised, as I was, at how many people are experiencing the same thing. And you will feel stronger for the discovery.

Photo Credit: Etienne Giradet

Lit Mag Love
An Interview With Editor and Podcast Host Rachel Thompson

Rachel was kind enough to reach out to me to be a guest speaker for her course Lit Mag Love. Lit Mag Love and her podcast, Write, Publish, and Shine, both give writers an edge in how to get those coveted acceptance letters. I think her work is such a great idea I wanted Rachel to share some of what she's learned with our readers.

Meredith Allard: How did you find your way to writing?

Rachel Thompson: Like a lot of writers, for me, it was an elementary school teacher who encouraged me after I wrote a poem for a class assignment. The poem was very earnest. But, looking back I realize it had internal rhymes and even some sixth-grade honesty/confessionalism in all that earnestness.

M.A.: Every writer has their own journey to publication. What was your journey to publication like?

R.T.: I wrote *Galaxy*, my collection of poems, over seven years and had the help of mentors and a community of writers during that time. And I published several of the poems in lit mags, which was a big learning curve. After I completed the manuscript, while I was in the Banff Wired Writers program, I sent it to a contest judged by a poet I admire greatly, Gregory Scofield. It was the first place I sent my manuscript; remarkably, I won! The prize was a paid publication contract with a small publisher, Anvil Press. Since then, due mainly to life events but also to challenges with confidence, I haven't created a second book. I've been working on a memoir for several years and am a slow writer. When I'm feeling my best, I embrace this slowness. For this reason, I have a mantra about writing to remind me to do it "in my own time and in my own way."

M.A.: Tell us about your experience as an editor at *Room*. What have you learned from being an editor?

R.T.: Being an editor at *Room* is an incredible privilege because I get to work in a brilliant and transformative community with amazing writers and editors. When I edited my first issue with Room (we are a collective of rotating editors), I chose the theme of grief because of the aforementioned life events, which were loss events. As I edited this issue, I gathered comfort and connection with other grievers, both the writers and our readers. It was really remarkable and I'll never forget how writing can do that—bridge people from lonely places to each other. (The most recent issue I edited was on the theme of neurodivergence and it did a similar thing.)

I continue to learn so much about writing by reading our submissions. It helps me hone into the difference between well-revised work from writers who are writing what they're meant to be writing and writing that needs more consideration and distillation. Though at *Room* we also work with writers who submit work that is almost there, especially when their voice isn't one we might have heard in literary journals.

M.A.: What is Lit Mag Love? How can it help writers who would like to be published in literary journals?

R.T.: Lit Mag Love is a five-week course I created that helps writers get a big "YES" for their writing from literary journals they love. In the course, writers learn how to submit writing more effectively and kick-start their writing careers with lots of care and support from me.

It is a course for writers who feel overwhelmed about sending their writing to journals and who get frustrated with the long waits, followed by the heartbreaking sting of rejection. The warm and supportive course community is the best part of the course.

M.A.: How can writers sign up for Lit Mag Love?

R.T.: The final session of the year starts really soon and you can learn more and sign up here: https://rachelthompson.co/litmaglove/. (If registration is closed, hop on the waitlist to be notified when it opens again.)

M.A.: Tell us about your podcast Write, Publish, and Shine. How is this podcast helpful for writers?

R.T.: The Write, Publish, and Shine Podcast is such a delight to create. I've been doing it for a few years now, and I feel so lucky to have had so many conversations with lit mag editors about writing, editing, and submissions. My goal with each episode is to give writers a-ha moments that will help them get published in lit mags. I hear from listeners who tell me it helped them overcome the fear of submitting their writing to journals and inspired them to submit to a journal they learned about in an episode.

M.A.: What is your best advice for writers seeking to be published in literary journals?

R.T.: When I work with writers who want to publish in lit mags, I always start with why. Why do you want to publish in lit mags? What are the qualities of lit mags that would help you reach your personal goal for publishing? Often writers submit to journals with only a vague idea about fit and no thought to how a publication might help them with their writing goals. Yet, the more focus you have on intentions and goals, the more likely you will meet them.

In the Lit Mag Love course, before we start researching journals to send their work, I help writers get clear on why they want to publish. We look at the most common reasons writers publish in journals and decide if one of these reasons most resonates with them and then build out a list of places to send the work.

It's always such a delight to see how that little shift in perspective helps writers feel more confident and clear about submitting and publishing their work. No longer are they sending out work to just anyplace that will have them. They choose the places that deserve their work.

M.A.: What else should our readers know?

R.T.: Keep following your own lights when it comes to your writing and submissions. You're doing great doing it your own way. You don't need to fit into anyone else's definition of success for your writing career.

I am on a social media hiatus for the first half of this year, but if you're reading this a little later in the year, you might find me on Twitter @rachelthompson and Instagram @rachelthompsonauthor. Meanwhile, feel free to email me at hello@rachelthompson.co if you have any questions about anything I shared.

HISTORICAL FICTION

Bethan Charles

Lisa Gordon

Benjamin Hulme

Richard Koman

Kim McCollum

Shannon Monroe

L.E. Smith

Amadea Tanner

Salinda Tyson

THE LOST DIARY OF EUNICE NEWTON FOOTE

By Bethan Charles

10th June 1856

Forgive the smudged ink, but I'm dripping with sweat, broiling under the ludicrous number of layers society demands I wear. I've shut myself in this oven for hours. Worth it, of course, because today, after weeks of effort, success.

The midday sun bathes my laboratory bench. On it, two glass receivers shimmer with heat, appearing innocent enough. Common air fills one, but unseen poison suffocates the thermometer trapped within the other. Isolating the carbonic gas took an age, and following my earlier failures, I had bent to defeat until dear Elisha helped build a most wondrous pump. We should patent it.

I digress.

My fascination lies not in the equipment but in the clues scribbled over the paper, drowning my desk – patterns in numbers. Science is a marvelous illusionist, disguising its simple tricks behind dazzling complexity, waiting for those with the patience to unravel its secrets. I found my patience in childhood, smuggling maple seeds into flower beds and watching giants grow from dirt, rooting questions within my mind. How does a tree fit inside a seed? Who planted flowers before people? Childish thoughts, of course, though the importance lies in the show of curiosity, not the questions themselves. At school, few teachers understood this distinction. They chastised my queries and willed me to join the other girls, learning in silence, but a handful of tutors broke expectations. My favorites inspired more questions, taught me to peel away the world's layers, exposing its truth, as I do now.

In navigating nature's entangled web, I'm uncovering its laws – simpler, fairer, more rational than those humanity conjures. And in my precious laboratory, I've discovered another. Carbonic gas holds more heat than common air.

But how? To what mechanism can I attribute this effect?

I'll admit, I am unsure and, during my musings, have nibbled the entire length of my pencil. A terrible habit, though no one is present to judge. This is my private space, a room that visitors with limited imaginations have dared call a closet. Elisha has his own office, and our girls avoid my endeavors. Mutinous adolescents. Despite my efforts, they show little interest in science, although Augusta is young. There is hope for her yet. She's reading outside, sheltering under the apple tree beside our arid flower bed. Our poor magnolias. They have no chance in this relentless weather.

I wonder.

Suppose the air contained more carbonic gas; would every summer day become as intolerable as this?

25th August 1856

Elisha thinks I should be grateful, but he is wrong. How dare Joseph dismiss my work's significance. In Albany, he declared, "Science has no sex," before summarizing my results as if I were incapable of speaking. I had not minded at first. After all, it honored me to hear my findings presented, but when Joseph questioned my experiment's value, I burnt with embarrassment, then fury. For Elisha's sake, I held my tongue for the rest of the meeting.

Afterward, Elisha defended Joseph. "He complimented you. Believed your experiments interesting."

Just not significant.

Elisha then had the nerve to question what I considered more important, the science or recognition? But why must that be my choice? Why not also his? I assured him that the audience would have understood if I had presented. They'd be in no doubt of my work's *significance*.

If the air contained more carbonic gas, our summers would be hotter. Shock choked me when the audience failed to gasp at this revelation. Perhaps the subdued reaction was because Joseph read my paper with his irksome monotony. I should have stood there, speaking with the fervor Elizabeth shows during our rallies. After telling Elisha this, he dared to reply, "The people would not have listened to you. Joseph gave your work a voice."

His words stung my heart despite their truth.

* * * * *

I waited our customary three hours before knocking on Elisha's office. When I entered, he remained glued to his armchair, peering over his spectacles in the way I despise.

"I already have a voice," I said with the passion I spent the afternoon practicing.

His beard twitched – his version of a smile. Others might believe he smirked, ridiculing my folly at thinking I was entitled to recognition. They would be wrong. He smiled with pride.

"Sorry," was all we said to each other.

The following silence lasted longer than usual. He broke it first, claiming I waited over three hours, but how dare he, of all people, question my timekeeping. I teased his tardiness, and he mocked my non-existent housekeeping. Afterward, we giggled like our girls. I've only just stopped.

13th September 1856

Elisha was right. Who would have heeded my voice? But Joseph's carried far, despite his restrained enthusiasm. The latest edition of Scientific American – no less – lies open beside me, with an article I can now recite from memory.

"The experiments of Mrs. Foote afford abundant evidence of the ability of woman to investigate any subject with originality and precision."

Recognition.

This journal credits my work, my results, my name. If a woman can unravel the laws governing nature, why can she not write the laws governing our land? Oh, I should remember that phrase for Elizabeth when I visit her. My achievement must be of note for the movement.

I should copy the article for inclusion in the next pamphlet. Every triumph propels our mission toward victory, vindication, votes.

1st October 1856

Elizabeth's response was reserved. Although she congratulated my success, her muted reaction deflated my jubilation. She reminded me, "The movement marches on with greater battles to win," as if my conquest was nothing more than a minor skirmish, insignificant in our war. I suppose that's true, though congratulations would not go amiss. During these darkening autumnal nights, motivation eludes me. At times, I wonder the point of continuing when so few people listen.

3rd November 1856

How does carbonic gas hold more heat than common air?

Re-focusing on this question has lifted my spirits and regenerated my purpose. Efforts with the movement have stagnated, but science continues, neutral in who unravels its mysteries. Next August, Joseph will stand before the association, lauding the value of my work. Or, perhaps, I'll speak.

29th December 1856

Fool. This is no laboratory. I am no scientist. I destroyed the glass receivers.

5th January 1857

Elisha replaced the broken equipment, despite my resistance. He is a stubborn beast.

2nd February 1857

Electrical excitation. Remarkable.

The work began as an accident. After exhausting the air from a glass tube, I received a frightful shock when touching its brass cap. I recruited Augusta to help dismantle the tube and find its broken component. But there was none. My resulting excitement confused her, though how my heart pounds when a new question arises. Where did the electricity come from?

Days of reading revealed this effect to be no novelty, although fascinating, nonetheless. Electrical currents can form by the compression and expansion of air. Intriguing, yes? In a fit of inspiration, I constructed the necessary apparatus in one night. These experiments are especially pleasing. Their occasional explosions frighten those blasted bluebirds nesting in the gutters. However, more than once, our girls have stormed in, claiming I'm disturbing their peace – to which I remind them, their entire childhoods disturbed mine.

20th August 1857

Elisha's beard twitched all day. When the meeting concluded, he said, "Don't forget me now you're famous." His pride fueled my joy enough to overlook that I sat as an observer yet again. Years might race but change dawdles, meaning the narrator of science remains as stubbornly male as our government. But, after the presentation, the audience flocked to me, interrogated me, congratulated me, not the man reciting my work.

Published twice this time. Twice. The timing's exemplary, considering how fast the movement now grows. My recognition will strengthen our cause. I have a voice, and I'll damn well use it.

10th June 1859

The movement stole two years. A worthy interlude, of course, though I have missed these four walls, this laboratory, equipment, notebook. I feel torn between many lives, each as vital as the other. At least our girls help with the campaign now. It transpires that they are fiercer than me, perhaps more so than Elizabeth. When I hear their voices shout at rallies, my heart burns warmer than the midsummer sun. Over the years, failure has stalked our movement, gnawing at my ambition. As our actions went ignored and our efforts were forgotten, I lost faith, but seeing our girls' passion grow inspires new hope.

Though I digress.

I must set aside my partisan nature, crucial if I am to restore my laboratory and decipher old notes. Nature's mysteries are easier to untangle with a neutral mind. Then I can drift, landing on the shores of answers too distant to imagine while tied to one spot.

It was Joseph who prompted my return. He wrote to me, checking I had kept recordings from the carbonic gas experiment – a curious request.

20th July 1859

Augusta sorted mountains of notes today. She was rather efficient, and I appreciated her efforts as I've felt overwhelmed since Joseph brought an article to my attention. A London man published a report, succeeding where I could not. He answered my elusive question – how does carbonic gas hold more heat than air?

Melancholy trapped me. I had failed. Three nights passed before I perused Joseph's letters again. Re-reading the reports he sent, it became clear the solution always lay beyond me. I laughed when I compared this London man's apparatus to my own. His methods mirrored mine though they reveled in the privilege granted by his position.

However much I adore my laboratory, I cannot escape it being a cupboard.

As summer marched on, I regained my sense. This man's experiment appeared to be built on mine, so I should be proud, despite how irritating I found his ignorance of my work. Besides, Elisha reminded me the lack of acknowledgment was likely an error. London is a great distance. We inhabit opposing orbits. So, I will compose my thoughts with my – now organized – notes and write to this man.

20th August 1859

No reply.

30th October 1859

No reply.

2nd January 1860

I've written again.

17th February 1860

Forgive my scribbled words. I tremble with fury. Enquires into this man's position revealed it likely that, years ago, he rejected my article for publication in the journal he edited. Yet, during a public address, he claimed nothing "as far as I am aware" was published on the topic I first studied!

I drafted five enraged letters before Elisha steadied my hand. The sentimental fool looped his arm through mine and listed my accomplishments while promenading me around our skeletal winter garden. I supposed it helped, at least enough to compose my thoughts for Elizabeth.

3rd March 1860

Elizabeth observes the world like a cloud, seeing past the horizon blinding those rooted in the earth. "You make mountains of molehills," she said. "Our purpose rises above your quarrel. Waste no more time on it." How I admire her ambition, although I sometimes feel lost in her shadow.

For now, I have retreated into my sanctuary – sorting the equipment littering my laboratory bench, connecting snippets of unfinished experiments. Science will calm my troubled thoughts. What question should I answer next? Ideas scatter my mind like the blossom sprinkling our garden, where Elisha sits reading in the shade. It is an absurdly glorious day for March. The sky, stained blue, tinged only with the smoke from the factory chimneys near the lake.

I wonder.

I'm curious to know the smoke's composition. Does carbonic gas mingle with the soot? How much? If one knew the number of chimneys in the world, one might estimate the weight of carbonic gas filling the air, then perhaps I could extrapolate my original findings. Intriguing. Now, how could I begin this? I wonder if—

I must go. Augusta wants help planting the seedlings.

THE BOSTON DOCTOR

By Lisa Gordon

"Don't look back," Nels said.

The gravity in his voice, her only comfort. The train ride had been long and unrelenting. Crowding in against countless others, Millie hushed Thelma, their new baby girl, so often her voice turned to gravel in her throat. The smell, unbearable: humanity at its worst. The persistent grumble of the tracks beneath them, the constant bump and jostle, a new torture. The only color, for so long, the backs of their eyelids.

"Almost there darling, almost there," Nels whispered, over and over, his eyes squeezed fiercely shut, his full lips pressed in a hard line. Who was he speaking to, she wanted to ask: her? Or Thelma? But she did not, she could not. That question was born of insecurity, and insecurity bred fear. Nels had taught her that; had taught himself that. And there was time for neither in their new life. She tightened her grip on the blanketed bundle of their daughter, and tried to imagine it:

Boston.

Nels had pointed to it on a map and told her it would be filled with bricks the color of persimmon and windows high in the starry sky. "All the medicine in the world is happening here," he'd said. "And we're going to be a part of it, yes, yes we are."

She loved him for that, how he included her, as if she, too, were taking a scalpel to someone's throat, or administering penicillin on the backs of dying tongues.

They arrived at Back Bay station to little splendor. The planks below her feet swelled with weight. Humidity clung to her skin like sweat. Immediately, the fashions affronted: swooping skirts, high-necked blouses, wide-brimmed hats. And the colors— oh! Colors Millie was not sure she knew the names of; colors of vegetables and fruits, perhaps, that didn't grow on her family's farm. Purples, greens, oranges bright as sunsets.

Thelma bucked in Millie's arms, silent, her eyes wild.

"We're here, baby girl, here we are!" Nels sang. His demeaner was back—another comfort she needed. He kissed Thelma's cheeks with lips pursed big and swollen. "Boston here we are!"

"*Shushhh*," Millie hissed, gripping his arm. But inside, she soared.

Nels pointed across the street. "There," he said.

"Where?"

"There!" Nels grinned, easy with the thrill of surprising her. "Our new apartment building."

"An apartment!" Millie said. "Nels!" She nearly dropped Thelma. The building stood before them, of quality Millie couldn't properly determine, but to her, it was wondrous.

"I promised," Nels said, taking her by the elbow and leading her across the tracks.

He had promised. It hadn't been her place to ask, but she had hoped; oh, how she had hoped! And now: an apartment of their very own. Their very own. It stood mightily, bricks upon bricks, just passed the station. Nels retrieved a key from his satchel, dangling it in front of her face, his smile enormous, infectious. The landlord, Nels said, had sent it two weeks ago. Gratitude and confusion—but how did he, when could he have—rushed to the surface of her cheeks. She kissed him, before remembering herself, then laughed, embarrassed.

Look at us, she thought, this new family, their new life. She couldn't get over the new smell of rust mixed with dry air, or the new sound of the train hissing, the porters calling out in their glossy voices, or the elegance of the ladies, the swish of their dresses. How quickly she came back to earth, the earth where they didn't belong.

Her Ma and Pa back home, her sisters and Uncle Rep: what would they say, if they saw her now?

The quarters were small and modest, but they were clean. A small mirror atop the mantle. An armchair in the corner, near the window. A straw bed, in the front room. A belly stove.

"We'll need to buy everything else, in due time," Nels explained. He set Thelma on the floor, shiny with wood polish. "My exams are next week. I expect to be employed soon thereafter."

What Millie wanted to say, she knew she couldn't. Was he certain the hospitals would hire him, here? Back in South Carolina, he'd gone to both local hospitals, dressed to the nines. He'd gone to many of the local physician practices, white and Black. He'd been turned away from every door. At first, his anger erupted like a rock thrown through glass. Then, it tempered, becoming more even, fueling his motivation.

He took Millie's cheeks in his hands. "I hope you are pleased, my darling," he whispered.

Millie squeezed the tears from her eyes, lest he see her cry. For he'd believe they were tears of joy. But once Nels left for the lay of the land, a strange sadness came over her—it had, perhaps, been there all along. He told Millie to rest, but she could not. From the window, she saw the wooden planks of the train platform, the steam hung in the air with a hot energy, the Boston skies grey and unwelcoming. People of the kind she knew nothing about on their merry ways, living their strange lives. Thelma fussing in her arms, her mouth a pink animal, wailing.

Millie watched her husband leave, thinking, when he came home, she'd have to find new ways to be a wife to him.

* * * * *

That first autumn, as the leaves fell and the sky stayed endlessly gray, Nels prepared for his licensing exam. Millie passed the time by taking walks with Thelma when she fussed. The accents were different in Boston. Clipped syllables, tight lips. She missed the sing-songyness of Southern talk, the rise and fall, how voices bloomed with vibrancy and anger, with gossip and laughter. She knew her accent marked her, but many other things did, too: the daughter of a former slave, she was also half white, a plantation owner's daughter, but too dark to pass. She'd feared she'd never match the Bostonian poise, a poise Nels already seemed to embody.

Millie preferred to the parks in the Commons to the commotion of the streets. Thelma loved the lake between the trees best, marveling at the big white birds gliding in the water. Later, she learned what they were: swans. She, too, was stunned by their majesty and elegance. She preferred to stay there as long as she could, but there was much to do at home. Walking briskly, she tried shed the imposter feeling as if it was weight she could lose.

Nels was late. Millie had barely anything other than barley and peas for dinner, and he was expected with their Sunday roast. She fretted at the window, trying to quell her eager stomach by sucking on rosemary leaves. She longed for a drink and wished she could ask Nels to bring some home, but knew how unladylike that was. Finally, he arrived with a parcel wrapped in newspaper.

"Today was grand," he said, kissing her on the cheek. "I shadowed Dr. Worthy all day. He's a fine man, indeed, and a finer doctor. He will help establish my practice."

"That's wonderful," she said. She opened the parcel and was surprised to find a rack of lamb.

"I thought you would like it."

"Oh, but we can't afford this!"

"It's on loan-away from the butcher. I'll pay back more next week."

"But your boards aren't for a few more weeks, and even then—"

"I'm going to be a doctor, Margaret. Here, in Boston. I am. And not a word of it again."

Nels' key had turned; he locked her door and was opening Thelma's, instead, reaching for her to hold her high in the sky, his smile as wide as her squeals of joy.

"I can't believe you'll be educated as a Bostonian," he murmured to her, burying his face in her neck.

She was envious of her own daughter, the very thing that sucked her dry of milk, of self. Envious of the life her daughter would lead. Envious of the love her husband showered her, copious, unbounded love. Her love for her daughter was love, yes. But it was rageful in its purity.

She opened the lamb, pressing her hands into its raw meat, realizing only then that she didn't know how to cook it.

* * * * *

Millie went to bed but couldn't sleep. She lay watching the candle burn out until Nels came barreling into the bedroom. He'd gone out with new comrades, at some saloon in Copley Square, drinking away money they still didn't have. She pretended to be asleep, but whether or not he knew that, he didn't let on.

"Millie-my-Margaret-my-lady-oh-my," he sang. "I've got it, I've got just the thing, the very thing indeed, indeed indeed indeed!"

Millie couldn't help but smile, though she kept it small and hidden in her face. Oh, how she did love seeing Nels like this, truly elated, walking on clouds, taking her along for the ride.

"The thing?" she said demurely.

He laid down in bed and kicked off his shoes with great labor—they toppled to the wooden floors Millie had cleaned hours earlier.

"*Sshhh*," she chided him. "Sometimes it's as if you forget you've ever had a daughter at all!"

"Oh, gracious me!" he cried, extending his arms beyond his head and grinning ear to ear. "As if I'd ever forget the love of my very life." He turned to her, his eyes bright and swimming.

Her skin sang, then quickly bristled, once she realized he'd not meant that she was the love of his life. At the same time, he caught his error, smart man that he was, even if drunk: "Second-in-standing, mind you."

"What, is it Nels?" she said, impatient now. She was jealous of the fun he was having, the fire lit in his brain.

"The thing," he said, "yes." He closed his eyes and rested his hand on her forearm. The rich, dark smoothness of his skin shone keenly in the candlelight.

"A hospital!" he cried.

"A...hospital," she said, not sure what he meant.

"My own, my very own."

"Your—your own? Your own hospital."

"Yes! Men have done it. A Negro man in Chicago. A Negro man in Georgia. Purchased small home dwellings and converted them into hospitals. Trained, Negro doctors. They've done it."

"But you've not yet—"

"It will be open to all patients. Anyone. Free of charge, if need be. And I will employ only Black physicians, and I will create a nurses's training program for young Black women, they need careers too, we need—"

"Impressive, Nels. But—"

"My sweet dear. I have responsibility. To forge it for others. To create opportunities for others. To raise us up."

"But Nels, you've not yet—"

"I will train them. I will give them jobs. He groaned, his body beginning to twitch.

"Donations will function here. We need to find a church." At that, he seemed to wake up, brightening. "Why haven't you found us our church?"

She hadn't known if Boston churches would be different from home. She hadn't known how to find out. "I…I don't know," she whispered.

He turned then, deciding to sleep, and this was a small gift. Millie had not yet said her piece—he had not let her. They both knew that he hadn't yet passed his boards. Nels knew that he would. Millie's uncertainty extended deeper than that. She was quite sure he'd pass his boards, but his larger plans frightened her. Not that he couldn't achieve them, but that she wouldn't grow with him. Wouldn't become the wife he'd need for such a life. That she wouldn't know how. She couldn't even find their church.

Tears came to her eyes. Luckily, they were only the beginnings of tears, tiny wells of water too timid to flow. She wiped them on the lace sleeve of her nightgown and began to undress her husband, who was snoring now, tumbling into dreams.

* * * * *

The house on East Springfield Street was unimpressive, but strong. And it was more than a house. A whole brick building of a thing—three, four floors from what Millie could tell.

Nels stood off to the side, watching her approach. "Well?" he said. Already impatient for her reply, though she'd just arrived.

Millie looked up and down. It was the same as the other rowhouses on the block, lined with early trees, forming a young canopy. "The street is quite lovely," she said, turning her head back to the building.

"The loveliness of the street is a side thought, if at all. Have you focused your attention on what's at the end of the block?"

Millie had not. Now she did. Beyond them lay the resplendent center pavilion of Boston City Hospital, its iron-domed pillared building just beyond view.

Nels reached into the bassinette and drew out his daughter, held her up, up, up. "Look!" he said. She made not a sound, but her smile disappeared into the sky.

"That's Daddy's, yours and mine, it's ours, baby girl!"

But it wasn't.

"It rings, Millie. It rings!" he exclaimed, circling the baby in the air, pointing her toward the city hospital, up and down the street, the building that might become his.

Ever the questions! Was it proper to have the city hospital a block away? Where and how would the patients find them? How would they pay? Who would he hire? Could they afford it? What about supplies? Was the city ready for a black physician? Were they? She bit her tongue, reminded of Nels' words: questions were born of insecurity, and insecurity bred fear.

But fearful, she was.

"So this will be just—"

"I will need somewhere to practice, Millie, in case they won't take me." He nudged his chin toward the hospital at the end of the block, its enormity looming. "I need somewhere to train others like me. I need to help us."

Oh, her good husband. Her good, courageous husband. She needed to chew her own fear and spit it out.

"You will, Nels. It could be—" Millie searched for words. "Revolutionary."

At that word, he seemed to deflate. He sat down on the front steps and settled the baby in his lap, her arms and legs squirming, wanting more of him. Millie watched his face, seeing this doubt upon him like a new skin. She knew she needed to scrub him clean of it.

She went to him and placed her palms on the sides of his head. She looked him in the eye, square as she could, and in them she saw two Corneliuses: one, the young man she knew so long ago, the dreamer; and two, the grown up version of that young dreamer, smoothing out his dreams like untangling a knotted rope.

"You will not just be good. You will be excellent."

He nodded back to the house. "If not I, someone else will do it," he said.

"Perhaps, though not as well."

She thought of him as a little boy, hauling coal into the fire of the McCrossin's home, his father out back chopping wood, his mother long dead; she thought of his tiny, capable hands, his brain, alive with fire, and how the couple admired him so much they paid for his schooling. They saw it in him, even then. (Sometimes, when she looked at Thelma, she thought: do I see that in her? Do I? And she thought: did anyone see it in me?) She thought of the letter from McCrossin that Nels kept in a cardboard file in his desk, next to the brass letter opener.

It seems to be but yesterday when you as a little boy was studying your Spelling book and performing your House-hold duties at our Home; how well I recollect the day you started to school and again I say that it fills my heart with pride to see that my advise has been kept by you and you have distinguished yourself at school and won a higher place than ever, in my friend-ship, I trust and predict that you will able, as a man of the world, to distinguished yourself among man-kind and do good for the race to which you have been born, there-by setting a fair example to the countless millions of your people.

"No one is as skilled as you," Millie said.

"But they are, Millie. I've good training, of course. But medicine is medicine."

"But medicine is not medicine. It is your touch, your manner, your temperance, that makes it so. Your confidence."

He looked toward the building again, gripping her fingers. "Perhaps that is why they won't follow my lead—" He turned Thelma toward him, cradling her in one arm, stroking her eyelids and nose with the light touch of a finger.

"No," Millie said, shaking her head slowly, side to side. "That is exactly why they will."

And, she wished she could add, *exactly why I have, too.*

* * * * *

He passed his medical licensing exam with flying colors. "Fireworks!" he said when he came home, his hands exploding in front of his face. "Fireworks!" As if saying the word made them appear. But, his eyes all lit up with stars and planets, his movements singeing with afterglow, she could almost smell the gun powder.

It seemed Thelma's tiny arms reached for him before he'd entered her vision. He flew her on his back, zooming about, singing me oh me oh my. Thelma's little giggles heaps of glee, dollops of creamed sugar fluffed on every other note, together their song becoming more familiar, yet more unpredictable, at once.

She wiped her hands on her apron. Back in the kitchen, Millie listened to the heady bubble of boiling water, the thud of the rolling pin on dense dough, until the sound of her own song became the only one she could hear.

LET THE WICKED FLEE

By Benjamin Hulme

The blade glided across my pale flesh; tiny hairs caught, severed at the stem to be taken and washed away. By the light of the candle, I dashed the water across my face and sat back with a sigh. The flame flickered, my shadow caught on the backdrop of my tent; how I wish you were here with me Ceilia, but then what horrors would I make you endure to have company this frozen night. Blood beaded to fall down my chin and land to dilute into the bowl, its metallic odor mixed with the stench of tobacco and whisky. I pulled at the blue wool of my coat; little good would it do me this night, for it was time to check up on the men. I checked I had my pistol and sword and pulled back the flap of the tent. Wisps of snow swirled, a harsh cold met my face, my boots were greeted by the compacted snow, which creaked under my weight, groaning with every step. There were few fires this night, orders from above, let the men freeze they might have said, or I suppose to be shot.

'Captain,' said Berkly. A small man but a strong one, he raised a hand to his cap and passed me by with a frown.

'Lieutenant,' I replied and walked on, past the many white rows of tents, the black forms of men huddled, watchful to the darkness of the night. Three men sat; slouched across their muskets, their dark blue coats masked by tiny motes of white. The narrow eyes of Sergeant Jim Shaw met me, he went to stand.

'At ease Jim.'

'Sir,' he replied.

The other two men cast me a sullen glance and returned their watch back to the wooded gloom.

'Ain't nothin' out there Sir,' whispered Issac. He was the younger of the three, young to the world and fresh off the boat. I took from my pocket my silver hip flask, a present from my Father, its face decorated with the flag of our country and beneath it an engraving, I could not see it for the darkness, but I felt with the frozen tips of my fingers across the indented words. They read PROUD FATHER. Would he be proud if he saw me now? To see where my commission had landed his only son. I tapped the flask to the side of Jim's shoulder, he looked up and smiled. He took it and screwed open the top, the metal touched his lips and the nectar dribbled down the blonde wisps of his beard.

'Thank you, Sir.'

'Leave some for the other boys,' I said, I leaned down and knelt beside him, keenly watching the twisted maze of branches across the field from our position. Isaac drank and then did Drew, a large Irish man, forever critiquing me on my pour choice of whiskey.

'It'll do Yankee,' he said in his thick Irish accent, his words partially muffled by the collar of his coat. He handed me the flask, I took it and drank; warm was my soul, all despair lost in an instant, to only return with the closing of the lid.

'Such quiet,' I said.

There was not a sound to be heard, the world muffled in a haze of snow, nothing but the heavy breath and sniffle of man. They listened; ears pricked, the faintest whisper on the wind, the distant creak of wood.

'Any news from up high Sir?' asked Jim.

'To sit and wait, that is all I have heard.'

'They are godless men to let us sit here and wait,' said Drew.

'There are few men in war who are graced with God Private,' I replied. 'Or in life,' said Jim.

I sat back and returned my flask to its pocket. Issac coughed, cleared his throat, and said: 'How can God let men kill Sir?'

'I think God is not responsible for the world here around us Issac, just the stars and the trees,' I replied. 'Think it not that we rule in his will, but we are unbound by our own.'

'Sir?'

'You're confusing the poor boy, Sir,' said Jim with a smile.

'Have you cut yourself?' asked Drew.

'I was shaving,' I replied, I felt up to my face and felt the sticky ooze of blood.

'Listen,' said Jim.

'Singing,' said Drew.

From the encampment drifted a voice, then another until all around joined in a chorus of singing. Amazing Grace; I felt a surge of joy, delight for the many voices that now met my ears. From across the white, there came, how sweet a sound, and now how we were found down here in the deepest depths of horror.

'Sing,' I said.

'What?'

'Sing.'

'My Lord has promised good to me-' they began.

'My word his hope secures, he will my shield and portion be-' I joined.

'As long as life endures.'

Everyone's voice lifted; Jim and Drew smiled at one another, their muskets at their sides as across the camp men took to the air and sang. 'My chains are gone-'

A crack broke the air, then a whistle. From the distant trees, flashes erupted, smoke rose to linger at the forest's edge. Jim ducked face down into the frozen earth, beside him Issac followed. I reached for my pistol at my side, I pulled back the hammer and fired, one shot and two, my bullets whizzing off to be taken by the white. I squeezed the trigger, nothing. I opened it to see that it was empty. I cursed. More shots whistled overhead.

'Return fire,' I shouted.

I caught Issac's eye, he hesitated, his fingers enclosed around the brown body of his gun. 'If you do not fire back you will die.'

Jim leveled his gun, aimed, and fired; a ball of smoke erupted as he recoiled back. Issac still lay, now flat on his belly, his eyes held shut.

I looked about me, trying to gauge some sense of the situation; further along the line, the next group of pickets were returning fire and to my relief, a flurry of blue coats, muskets in hand were emerging from behind the many tents. Jim let off another round. Shots cracked the air around us, a haze of fire, thick white smoke billowed to cover the field. Drew was dead. He must have been hit first, he lay where he had sat, slumped forward, his musket still rested across his lap. God rest his soul. I fell to my knees and crawled towards Drew's body, the frozen snow, and soil filling between my nails and fingers. I retrieved his leather ammunition pouch and slung it over my shoulder. Beneath his body, the snow had already taken on a pinkish hue, a halo of red slowly seeping to fill in the grooves of the earth around him. I prised the weapon from his grip and leveled it, it was heavier than I remembered. My fingers tightened on the trigger, I fired, my world obscured by a cloud of smoke. 'K Company, form a line.

'Get up boy,' said Jim.

'I can't,' replied Issac.

A man to my left cried out and fell back clutching his chest. Jim fired another round off toward the trees. Another boy who I recognised as Will had been hit, he wailed, clutching at his stomach, his entrails slithering into the world like a lamb in spring. 'Mother,' whispered Issac.

I removed a cartridge from the pouch at my hip and tore it open with my teeth. I poured it down the barrel, dropped the ball, tapped the butt of the gun onto the earth, pulled back the hammer, and leveled. Small shapes of men hung at the edge of the distant forest, hidden by smoke and trees. I set my sights on one such shadow and squeezed. I was deafened by the noise, smoke covered my face and hair. I did not see or know of his demise, but repeated the act; I removed a cartridge from the pouch at my hip and tore it open with my teeth. I poured it down the barrel, dropped the ball, tapped the butt of the gun onto the earth, pulled back the hammer, and leveled.

I fired.

Issac had stood, how he trembled, he lifted his gun and fell back, a bullet in his gullet, he wrathed and struggled, gasping for air and then fell still. God.

Innocence, whether one way or another, is often the first of casualties in war. I removed a cartridge from the pouch at my hip and tore it open with my teeth. I poured it down the barrel, dropped the ball, tapped the butt of the gun onto the earth, pulled back the hammer, and leveled. I fired. Around me, more men were beginning to file into form a line, their Sergeants, and Corporals bellowing orders for them to fire.

'Poor kid,' said Jim. He leveled his gun. Smoke erupted into the air as he fired once more. 'Bastards.'

I caught my breath, my cheeks were singed as were my fingers. The blue, red, and white hung limp, falling from the pole that was lifted high above the thin blue line. A ragged bunch of boys and men, they stood and fired. Around them lay the many dead and dying, a scattered mass of limbs and broken bodies.

'Company K, fix bayonets,' shouted one of my Lieutenants, I had given the order as the fighting had subsided. We would see them off, to run and never return. Jim nodded my way, his face had blackened, his hair mangled by sweat, stuck across his skull.

'Should we not secure our position, Sir?' asked Lieutenant Berkly, he held his pistol at his side, he struggled to regain his breath. A shot whistled by and he took a step back.

'We will see them off, now organize the men, we will advance in file.' 'Is it not foolhardy-'

'See to your men Lieutenant,' I said.

I stood beside Issac's body; his pale hazel eyes once so full of life, now empty. I prayed he was with God now. I lifted my sword and cut down through the air and as one, my men lurched forward, one boot at a time, steadily to march toward our enemy's death. I glanced either side of me; blackened cheeks and wild stares, I guessed we still numbered almost sixty, we could still win this. From out of the trees; horses snorts and cries from wounded men drifted on the wind, few remained if any but to fire off the odd crack of musket fire. I prayed that they had fled and that we could all return to the warmth of our beds to dream of our loved ones. My thoughts returned to Ceilia, her soft skin, pressed upon mine as we lay, soaked in the dull wash of candlelight. Our naked forms, wrapped in an embrace. Would she be sat now, looking out from our home in Boston, as the gentle snows drifted down from the heavens to settle on the cobbles?

'Steady,' said a Sergeant.

I breathed, in and out, my breath catching on the walls of my throat. 'Steady,' I heard myself saying.

Buckles and straps chinked, boots pounded the hard ground as muskets knocked together. Men cleared their throats, another let out a sob, we marched on into the winter gloom. My heart pounded. I was a fool.

'K company halt,' I shouted. The company came to a halt.

'Halt,' barked the voices of my officers. This was a mistake, we should turn back.

'Sir?' asked Berkly.

I waved him back with my hand.

'Let me think,' I replied.

I could see little of the coming trees, we were almost amongst them. A red-breasted bird; a robin hopped along the snow-covered earth, it stopped beside a patch of red and then took off.

'Sir?'

'We will advance Lieutenant, send word to Bill to watch our left flank.' He nodded and replied: 'Yes sir,' he turned and barked an order.

I must keep my head.

'Company, forward.'

Again the body of men moved onward, the snow creaking under their boots. The black mass of uniformed men stark against the white.

'Steady,' said Jim.

The sword handle felt clammy in my palm, sweat smeared the surface of my skin. One foot after the other, head lifted, I stared into the bleak void from under the peak of my cap. I could see them now, apparitions at the edge of the forest.

'Company halt,' I shouted.

The company came to a stop.

Muzzles flashed between the looming trunks; a man fell to my side, a red cloud between us. 'Take aim.' A shot whistled through the air.

The men aimed. 'Fire.'

Crack went the muskets, white smoke erupted to billow up to the heavens.

'Chargeeeee.'

I looked up; my men were firing off wildly at the retreating men. One who had almost escaped stopped, cupped his hand to his side, and fell back, much to the cheers and hollers. We had won, but at what cost. I looked down at Jim; his fingers still around my own, his dark eyes stared up blankly into the white above. 'Be free Jim.'

We formed up and returned back to camp, we gathered our dead and wounded, but left theirs for the crows. It pained me; for they too, were someone's father or son, brother or uncle, Lover or Husband, and there they lay, still, cold and by morning they would be gone, covered by the snows and then the next. Crude crosses marked the graves of Sergeant Jim Shaw, Issac Smith, and Drew O'Connell, but I would remember them, and the other twenty-three men that died with them.

Bayonets lowered, my sword in hand, we charged. We passed between the bodies, scattered amongst the scrub and through our smoke to be met by the survivors of our volley. My legs were a blur beneath me, my breathing heavy, I kept my head low until I looked up into the wild eyes of a man, his hands dragging a wounded comrade. I hacked down and thrust through his grey coat until I felt the steel slip between the flesh and bone of his side; he recoiled, his hands fell away from his friend and he fell back to be taken by the onrush. I could smell the beer on his breath, it had escaped between his crooked yellow teeth, which were now clouded with red. Muskets fired, bayonets were thrust. Blood covered the earth. Cries for mercy and of Mothers filled the air. They were running now, crawling, scrabbling to escape us. A shot rang out. And to my side I saw Jim, he staggered, his musket fell to his feet and he slumped down, I reached out and caught him between my arms. He looked up at me and whispered: 'Shit.'

I gently lowered him down, my arms held tightly about his body; his hand spiraled in the air in search of contact. I took his hand in mine and squeezed. 'Nancy.'

'She's with you Jim, we all are,' I whispered.

My vision blurred, I could feel the hot fall of tears on my cheeks.

'I don't want to go, Sir.' He squeezed my hand.

Blood slipped from between his lips to pour through the fair wisps of his beard. He smiled, his eyes searching for some meaning, they found mine and he nodded. 'He is here now.'

And he was gone.

'Sir?' It was Berkeley. 'They are retreating.'

'Let them go, -let them go.'

TRUE FRIENDSHIP

By Richard Koman

SEPTEMBER 1906. IN THE AFTERMATH OF THE GREAT EARTHQUAKE AND FIRE, San Francisco needs honest leadership. Unfortunately, her mayor is Eugene T. Schmitz. And the city is absolutely controlled by "the little boss," Abraham Ruef.

"San Francisco is too small a stage for him now," Abe explains to Big Jim Gallagher as they slurp oysters in the little boss's private dining room.

Jim interrupts the carving of a roast to pour whisky from a crystal decanter.

"Just have a drink, Abe," Jim says. "You need it tonight." Abe demurs at first then allows the pour, to Jim's surprise.

"We were walking here, to the Pup, and he's explaining it to me, he's going to talk to the Kaiser himself about the German insurers denying our earthquake claims. Oh, he'll make a grand tour of it, visit all the crowned heads of Europe. When what do we hear?"

"Yeah?"

"Fucking cheers. A cable car passing us and the whole car of bastards are cheering him on."

"Even though he shot the quake looters without warning."

"Well, he beams at that, turns to me and says, 'You see, Abe? A great man needs a great stage.' He'd have no stage without me."

"All the world's a stage," Big Jim says. "Why not here as there?"

But it's at that moment the doors fly open and Loupy himself wheels in a cart full of silver trays. With an endlessly repeated flourish, Loupy reveals baked trout with anchovy sauce, stuffed lamb, roasted duck, leg of mutton, four dozen raw oysters, and an explosion of Dungeness crab.

"What is this, Loupy? We don't need all this."

"Oh I know, Monsieur Abe, but the mayor ..."

Abe furrows a brow. "He's been upstairs? How long?"

"Quite a little while, Abe," Loupy says but he doesn't withdraw. "Something, Loupy?"

"The liquor license, Abe. The city says they won't renew."

But Abe just shrugs. "I don't work for the city. I'm just a private attorney."

"If you were my attorney, though?"

"I would be a zealous advocate. Come to the office in the morning." "Oh yes, thank you, Abe. Thank you."

The laughter of young women cuts off the conversation. Men roar with drink and girls giggle. Bustling into sight is the familiar but extraordinary presence of Eugene T. Schmitz.

Gene, raven haired with an equally black beard, exudes comfort and privilege and sex appeal. Frank Mastretti, in Abe's opinion, is a back- stabbing son of a bitch but Abe will deal with him. Gassy Kelly is usually drunk and tonight is no exception. And, of course, always, there's a bevy of pretty whores, champagne bottles in hand.

A girl runs her fingers through Gene's massive black beard and lingers her fingers on his chest. He sends her off to sit with Abe.

Joining him, the girl giggles, "He's so short ..." But she buries her soft head into his shoulder, her hand sliding to his thigh.

"That's all right," Abe moves her hand off his thigh.

"Abe doesn't care for the ladies," Maestretti laughs. But when he catches Abe's eye he shuts the fuck up.

"Come sit with Big Jim," Gallagher offers, and soon enough has a whore on each of his massive thighs.

"Well did you tell him, Abe?" Gene asks.

"I was about to," Abe says crossly.

"You're the new mayor!" Gene exudes.

"Acting mayor," Abe clarifies.

Big Jim gulps down an oyster before he has to spit it out. Abe sips his whisky with distaste.

Gene smiles broadly and kisses a whore.

* * * * *

ABE WAKES WITH THE DREAD OF EMPTINESS UPON HIM, A FEELING OF being stuck in the world. He wakes ravenous, only to discover it's the middle of the night.

He cannot go back to sleep but feels he cannot wake. Gene is leaving and Abe is left in a nether world between living and dying.

Abe recalls being 10 years old, in his father's store, pouring kidney beans and cornmeal into bulk containers. He watches his father and recalls the cool, pale touch of his hand. Seems like a ghost, even then. Decides on a way out -- riding his good- boy boy-grades like a steam train across the Bay to Berkeley and back to Hastings Law.

Abe rises silently in the dark, pads his his way to the kitchen. As he heats the cast iron pan, glistening with the freshness of oil, he can almost see his future. As he cooks the inner organs of beasts and fowls, he recalls the first compromise and first betrayal. The meat sizzles and Abe fully understands that the betrayals never stopped and would never stop.

He grabs a metal tongs to flip the sausages, pork chops, and eggs. Staring at the blistering of the meat, he too is muscle and bone and sinew and blood. He feels the animal body of that but his heart beats so quietly he wonders if he even has one.

Abe dresses quickly, elegantly, knotting his tie and fastening the diamond stick pin he got from Bassity a long-ago night when they talked over the body of a dead girl. A good soldier then, Abe made the girl disappear and the King of the Underworld suffered no pause in the commerce of misery. Those were the sorts of compromises one made on the path to power. Having power, he could scarcely complain about the compromises. He wears the diamond pin, if he's honest, as a remembrance of shame. An emotion rarely felt now but in the memory of feeling.

* * * * *

IN 1901, DRAYAGE COMPANIES LOCKED THE TEAMSTERS UNION OUT AND brought in scabs. There ensued a violent fight on the docks that led to a city-wide General Strike. When the union prevailed, they created their own political party, the Union Labor Party.

"The psychology of the mass of the voters is like that of a crowd of small boys or primitive men," Abe explained to Gene in '01. "Other things being equal, of two candidates they will almost invariably follow the fine, strongly built man."

The election was looming and Abe had a wild, insane idea. The bastard bosses had tried to crush the union and been broken by the determination of men who refused to buckle. Determination plus brass knuckles and tire irons. Father Yorke had boiled the resentment on high until the party was born. Now it needed a leader.

Abe, skilled politico for 20 years, had the moment in hand. He had the steed, just needed to guide him into the starting gate.

"I have no ability to act as mayor. I have no experience. I don't know anything about city affairs. The whole thing is preposterous."

Abe said some things about experience and knowledge being overrated before he got to the heart of the pitch.

"You are a man of fine appearance. You are tall, well built. If you are nominated, people will naturally turn as you pass and say, 'There goes the Labor candidate for mayor.' At the theatre you will have a thousand people talking about you every night and advertising you, who scarcely give you a glance now. Think it over. I see a chance of making a big man of you."

Abe's eyes wandered over Gene's physique. Tantalizing, forbidden images floated through Abe's mind. Dangerous thoughts, which Abe pushed away. And then they came upon a gypsy woman with a little table set on the corner of Market and Kearny. Strange to find her, didn't Abe think? In the midst of the great city, throbbing with life and streetcars and newsboys and the parade of men in black suits and black hats and women strangely transformed through the latest corset-wear.

"Passing strange," Abe agreed, "but let's see what she says." And Gene pulled up a wicker chair right there on Market. The woman asked Gene where he was born.

"Right here! San Francisco is my native city."

She spread out a deck of ornate cards and told Gene to select three. Gene was not the only one whose breath caught a little to see what Lady Fortune might hold.

The Five of Pentangles. He saw crippled beggars walking through the snow. They pass a church but the doors are closed. "But you see it's upside down," the gypsy said. "The poverty you see will become riches. The doors that are closed shall open."

Four of Wands.

The card showed garlands and wreaths and a man and a woman draped in cloth and waving bouquets. They stood before a castle but the perspective was from some distance.

"There is a great celebration coming soon. You shall embark on a great enterprise and riches shall befall you," the woman pronounced. "Do you know of anything like this in your future?"

Gene was flabbergasted and speechless. "I -- I --"

The Queen of Cups.

She looked at the card a long while. Sighed. And pronounced. "Listen, you shall hold a high and mighty position in your native city." Gene lit up with white light.

"But hear me," she said. "This queen is the nurturing mother. This queen lives within you. Do not harden your heart to her. Do not forget women. If you live only in the world of men, evil will befall you."

But Gene heard nothing she said after she pronounced him mayor.

"I'm not superstitious," Gene told Abe, "but you can't buck against a hunch like that!"

* * * * *

NOVEMBER 1901

The miracle was delivered in the early hours the morning after the election. After Julia Schmitz raised her husband from the dead, the new mayor and the new boss sat in the basement den in comfortable leather chairs.

Abe leaned forward in conspiracy.

"The gypsy is not the only one has visions of the future, Gene," Abe whispered.

"I see the Union Labor Party as a spark lit in California that will kindle the entire nation and make a Labor president! I see the Union Labor party as a throne for you, as mayor, as governor, as President."

Gene bathed in the light of ambition.

"Behind that throne I see myself, its power, local, state, national. ... Looming in the distance, I see myself a United States Senator."

And what would my father think of that? he thought. The father who was always looming in the past.

Gene rose to his feet, stuck out his hand, then grabbed Abe in a bear hug. Finally, they raised glasses of champagne.

"Eternal fealty," they pledged as their glasses clinked.

SEPTEMBER 30, 1906

Gene's last supper in San Francisco, at least his last unwashed in shame, is a raucous affair. He sits at the center of the head table, Abe on his right hand, Big Jim Gallagher on his left. All the supervisors are there, 18 of them.

Reporters, too -- Scoop Gleeson, Livernash, a girl named Barstow and all the ink-stained wretches.

The scene is cheery and well-lubricated. After the obligatory clang of fork on glass and the long ramp down from static to silence, Gene rises to give his speech.

"Honored and dear friends. From the bottom of my heart I thank you for your wonderful, loyal service since the great fire destroyed our fair city. I am going abroad to study civic government in the great capitals of Europe, to probe problems of municipal ownership and perhaps to resolve our German insurance claims.

"I am leaving the office of the municipality in good hands. Mr. Gallagher is a gentleman whose loyalty to the administration has been tested on the firing line."

Of Gallagher's loyalty, Abe has no doubt.

"I have not asked him to do anything in particular. I have not attempted to outline a policy for him to pursue. I will leave it to him to decide on his own policy, which I know will be in line with the interests of the people."

Here not even Abe can resist a smirk. Catches himself and revives his straight face. Reminds himself, he is too smart, too self-aware for his own good. His father's voice again.

Gene stands and lifts a glass. Abe joins him. And Big Jim. All of the supes and hangers-on and even the reporters.

"To Gene! To the Mayor!" the toasts begin before Gene begins his flourish. "In conclusion, I want to say this: I am not a politician. I do not do things for political reasons. I do what I think is right and best and in the interests of my friends. My friends are my friends for personal reasons and not for political ones -- not because they have power but because they are dear to me!"

The reporters laugh hysterically at this but Abe ponders. Did Gene truly think that Abe was dear to him? They pledged eternal fealty but what did it mean now that Abe stopped dangling the governorship before his protege? Far harder times were coming, Abe knows.

Gene turns to Abe and bows. They all drink deeply and light cigars but Abe lips the glass and declines a cigar.

Now it is time to send Gene the message. The supervisors will genuflect and Gene should listen closely to what they say. There will be only passing praise for the once and future leader of the City.

The supervisors are sad to lose their beloved mayor, Big Jim declares. "But I shall have the opportunity to carry out the policies of our beloved mayor and I am thankful that I shall have the assistance and advice of his attorney, Abe Ruef, to guide me."

"When I was elected supervisor," drummer Sam Davis says, "the mayor told me all he wanted me to do was do what was right and I have always followed his advice."

Sam insists on more champagne for all.

"All this gabble about a split up between the mayor and Abe here is a lie!

There they are - brothers, as close as ever they were. The people of San Francisco ought to be glad to Abe Ruef for he has done for them!"

Thunderous applause, in which Abe politely joins.

No one could understand drunk Gassy Kelly and he soon slinks back down into his seat.

But the dentist Charlie Boxton confesses: "There have been times which I was tempted to stray from the right path. Such moments come to all of us. But every time that has happened Abe Ruef was always at my side to tell me what was right and what was wrong, and steer me in the right direction."

Three cheers for Abe! Boxton demands. When the cheers were done, Abe stands. The room quiets for the boss's benediction.

"There is nothing in life more exalted than true friendship," he says. And he looked almost kindly at Gene.

* * * * *

STRIPPED OF HIS PROTEGE, HIS STEED, HIS BROTHER, ABE WALKS UP town, through the still-ruined wreckage of the Earthquake. Up Kearney towards North Beach, the water, the Barbary Coast.

He walks along Pacific, passing gas-lit saloons and whorehouses and sailors rolling in the streets. He finds a hidden alley unknown to the tourists, where no one would shake his hand or clap his back.

He follows a pale light at the end of the alley to a secret, shameful window. He watches almost-naked boys in sequined g-strings dance in the red lights.

He does not go in. Just stands in the shadows and watches with his hand in his pocket. Tomorrow he will send Gene off on his ship to the crumbling old empires. Tomorrow Abe will rebuild his empire.

Tonight, if only for one brief moment, he will simply be alone, utterly alone and fully at peace.

BOOTLEG BETTY

By Kim McCollum

Mama leapt from bed as the lonely bellow of the train whistle sounded in the distance. Woot, whoop, whoop. The baleful sound pierced the pale, purple morning sky three times. Three gallons this time. She had erected a small hen house at the edge of our property closest to the Butte, MT train station. I knew that is where she was headed. She could use my help, but I wasn't allowed to accompany her. Too dangerous, she said. If it was too dangerous for me, it must be too dangerous for her as well, I thought. This wasn't a fight I could win, however many times I had tried.

Mama still brewed her hooch in our kitchen, but she sold it in the hen house for two reasons. One, to hide her hooch from the cops, and two, because the men who came to her were not gentlemanly, so she didn't want me around them. Before she put up the hen house they used to come to the house. I was only ten years old, but I knew something wasn't quite right. The men always made me feel uncomfortable.

"Well, hey there, Bootleg Betty," they'd say. "How's about a gallon of that sweet whiskey for me and my buddy here. We had a long week and could use a bit of your smooth fire water to calm the nerves." They would remove their hats covered in soot and dirt and place them on our clean kitchen table. The smell of them, tobacco, sweat and leather, would linger in our home for hours after they left. Some of them even lit a bit of the moonshine on fire to check the color of the flame. Mama explained that some bootleggers tried to make cheap, quick liquor with gasoline or paint thinner which could kill a man. If the flame burned orange, the hooch was pure. Blue meant poison. Mama's brew was always pure. The bright orange flame lit the men's eyes with desire. But the worst was the way they looked at Mama.

"When'd you say your man was returning?" they'd ask.

"Not sure exactly," Mama replied, even and smooth. She told me that no man would believe that she and I survived out here all alone, so they bought her lie.

Most of Mama's customers worked for the Northern Pacific Railway, so the hen house's location near the train station made sense but lugging the pints and gallons across the bumpy acres to the hen house was a time-consuming ordeal. Each jar was wrapped in cloth and set upon hay in the back of the wagon to prevent breakage. That was my job. When one broke, Mama would deduct it from the money I got to spend in town, so I painstakingly wrapped each one. Pints were sold for fifty cents, gallons for two dollars, so they were precious cargo.

Our neighbor, Helen, was concerned for us. Mama was becoming famous. The name "Bootleg Betty" was heard on the lips of many in town. Helen came by less frequently.

An urgent rapping at our door startled us awake one morning. Bundled against the cold, her eyes peering from beneath her hat and above her scarf, Helen stood rubbing her mittened hands frantically against her skirts.

"May I come in?" she asked, looking over her shoulder.

"Of course," Mama said, ushering her inside. Mama added fire to the stove and set the kettle on the burner.

"I'm afraid I can't stay," Helen began. "I just came to warn you."

Mama stopped stirring our porridge and turned to face Helen. "Oh?"

"I heard a rumor that the Federal officers are on to you," Helen said. "They raided Josephine's place in town yesterday. They gave her a warning and fined her $50. Not a terrible punishment, if you ask me, but that was just a warning. They said if they catch her again, she'll go to jail."

"I appreciate you coming to tell me, Helen. I know how you feel about all of this. You'd better get going. I don't want to put you in harm's way," Mama said, shooing her out the door. "Simone, open the windows to get some air in here. I'll hide the still."

As we sat down to eat our breakfast, a heavy knock at the door made me jump. Mama leaped from her chair but stopped before opening the door. I could see she was breathing deeply.

"Hello," she said, her voice smooth, betraying nothing. "Can I help you gentlemen?"

A tall man in a worn blue uniform removed his hat and held it against his thigh. He had thin sprigs of hair not unlike that of a baby. I thought it made him look much less professional.

"Rumor has it that you've got yourself a side business," he said.

"I'm not sure what you mean," Mama said.

The man lifted his nose into the air and said, "Smells like you've got a batch of hooch brewing as we speak!"

"I-I," Mama's calm began to crack.

"I was making pancakes," I said.

The man chuckled and looked down at me. "Is that so? Could I try one?"
My heart leapt in my chest as I thought what to say next. "I'm awfully sorry, sir, but I ate the last one."

Mama's eyes bore into me. The man eased himself onto one knee in front of me. His face was so close that I could see the pores of his skin and feel the heat his breath as he spoke.

"You know it's against the law to lie to an officer, don't you, young lady?"
My throat was tight, and I swallowed hard, but said nothing.

"There seems to be a misunderstanding," Mama said.

The man rose and put his hat back on his head. "Tell you what. I've heard you have the best hooch in town from more than one mouth in town. I'd hate for this here young lady to lose her Mama, so I'll make you a deal."

Mama put her hands on my shoulders and pulled me into her. She waited for him to continue.

"You hand over your hooch and I'll let you go with a warning." The man paced and tapped his bottom lip with his forefinger as he talked. He stopped and pointed at Mama. "I'll have you know that this is the only time you'll get off this easy. If I find out you've hidden bottles away or that you're brewing again, you'll do time. You understand?"

Mama nodded, lifted the mattress of our bed, and revealed at least a dozen small bottles stashed near where our feet lay at night. I had never even known they were there.

"Simone, help me gather these for the officer. Careful not to break them."

The officer shook his head and chuckled. "You women sure think you are sly. Sleeping with your child on a bed of hooch."

Mama's cheeks colored as she wrapped the bottles in cloth and handed them to the officer. I started towards the door to head out to the hen house, but Mama grabbed my shoulder. My head shot around to stare at her. She shook her head almost imperceptibly.

"Y'all have a good night, now," the officer said as he turned and headed out the door.

It seemed I could hear our hearts thumping in the stillness he left behind.

"Mama," I said when I was sure the man was far enough away. "Why didn't you tell him about the hen house? You heard what he said about jail, right?"

"Shhhh, Love," she said, wrapping her arms around me and planting a kiss on my head. "It'll be alright. He got what he really wanted. If he returns, it will be the same story. He'll like my hooch, so that's what he will be after."

"But what if you're wrong? What if you go to jail? What will happen to me?"

Tears flowed freely now down my cheeks and onto my shirt.

"Butte likes its drink. The officers are no exception. They let moonshiners off with warnings, small fines, and pints. Don't you worry. We'll be fine," she said holding my head against her chest.

Mama was right about the officers. They came often and demanded more pints each time, but we had enough to keep them quiet. 1912 was the best year of my life. We had plenty of money, Mama was happy. She and Frank had developed more than a friendship and despite my initial reservations when he asked me for permission to marry my Mama, I acquiesced. I saw how happy she was when he picked her up to take her to the dance hall from time to time. I didn't want Mama to miss out on another chance at love.

She died before they had a chance to marry. One of my most difficult memories is the image of strong, capable Frank crumpling to the floor and sobbing with his head in his hands when I went to him after I found Mama, her beautiful face gone when her whiskey still exploded, that horrible day. I had always hoped I'd find a man who loved me like that. Mama was lucky to have known that love not just once, but twice. It didn't matter that she had lost those loves. She had known love so strong that it made her untimely death almost bearable.

THE SECRET HISTORY OF THE GREAT KHAN'S SHADOW

By Shannon Monroe

She fought to move her body forward and prevent its decline to the ground, but its movement was as inevitable as a stone held aloft that ever seeks its soiled mates below. Once she had half-walked, half-crawled into the tent, she collapsed beside Bilgeh on her carpets of fine knot and weave, her lips pressed together. She sat in the north and faced the fire before them. It simmered and crackled beneath the bronze cauldron. Bilgeh drew his legs close, still uneasy in the presence of his new patron. Her eyes, ever suspicious, raked the young man's face for a sign of confidentiality, then she surrendered to his question.

"Are you the shadow? Are you the Great Khan?"

And she spoke.

"When Temujin first came forth his fists were clenched, and blood seeped between his tiny fingers. Our grandmother pried them apart and cried out. Mother, bleary eyed and exhausted, was suddenly revived from the midst of her pains. Grandmother held the Omen aloft––a blood clot––a sign of destined greatness. 'See, Hoelun, what I told you!' When I was brought forth two minutes later, no blood clots graced my wrinkled palms, but therein converged my own lines of fate, mirrored in the palms of my brother.

Our mother's sister acted as our wet nurse to satiate the endless demand for sustenance, a demand much greater than that of our siblings and cousins. We were much too loud for the ger,[1] where every cry and shriek and babble could be heard from but a few feet away. Mother tied small leashes to the lattice wall to keep us at a distance from the fire.

 We grew bigger, and quicker, and our shoes became tight. None could tell us apart, Temujin and I. We had the same round face with reddened cheeks, the same earnest eyes, the same mouth, and nose. Our hands looked more the same than even our faces. One summer day, I offered to trade with him, and he looked eagerly upon this idea, and nodded.

At my instruction, we each crossed our arms and joined hands, right to left and left to right. Temujin asked to make up the vow, and I agreed. Perfectly at eye level, he spoke. "My hands are your hands, in this secret we live." I repeated after him. We held somber appearances for a short moment, and then I saw the corners of his eyes twitch slightly. We broke down in laughter all at once, breaking our grasps and clutching our sides with giggles, now each using the other's hands.

I looked often at my brother's hands, now down at my side, now clutching the bow, now waving at our grandmother in the distance. When, at age eight, Temujin fell from his horse and cut his right hand on a jagged rock, I picked it up and did the same to my own. The attacks on his breath were less frequent then, and our father still walked upon the steppe.

We were cast out in winter after Mother had been taken captive, and father had been poisoned. There was little food to eat. We chewed on grass roots and pulled insects from the ground to keep the hunger at bay. We urged our falcon onward to hunt, but she did not wish to obey such wastrels as we had become. We were captured in spring and set to the plow as oxen in the enemy camp. I could never see it on my own body but observed that Temujin was slightly hunchbacked for years after, and his head bent forward at an unnatural angle. Thick calluses formed on our hands and shoulders.

One day we had earned enough praise from our pull that we were given a strip of mutton fat to share. Our elder brother yanked it away from Temujin, and I watched silently as my twin drew his knife and struck. We were twelve years old when we piled stones upon Elder Brother's body and told our siblings that he had been kicked by an unbroken horse. We were ashamed that the fat still tasted so good.

When we saw the great wolf of the world, things changed. Upon the vast steppe she stood, out of sight of our siblings and mother, who was now returned to us. The wolf gave me her steps, and her fangs. When Temujin saw her, he fell as if struck. He was moved much more deeply than I, and he cast out the dogs from our camp in fear, insisting instead that I and our siblings guard it––day and night. He would have no howling beast near his bed.

All the same, despite this terror of dogs, I watched his tenacity grow tenfold in the ensuing year. My skill and his spirit meant good food every night; even without dogs, we became fine hunters. Our family drank sour erok[1] and roast mutton, earned by trading pelts with merchants, and these comforts to our bellies held fast even when a new winter dragged on, and the crackling white snow was peppered with dung heaps.

Temujin went to live with the family of Borte when we were sixteen, and never had I felt so alone. Our siblings were always one step behind us, and without him I was restless, with nowhere for my thoughts to go. However, after he had performed his apprenticeship, the engagement was ended, and his marriage approved. I could see him with frequency again.

Borte surprised me. Stern she was, and very tall. When she was carried off in a raid, I remember being surprised. Temujin called upon me to help him recover her. We rode through the night and slew many in the enterprise. We regained

Borte, and word began to spread that our family hid baatars. I puffed up in pride.

With this reputation, it was easy to establish a quda for our youngest sister. When her bridegroom asked to forego the apprenticeship, however, I nearly drew my bow.

Temujin spat on the ground and grabbed the man's arm. He wished to pay for our sister, rather than train in our ways? He wished to substitute a coin where there should be a scar? It was unacceptable. Instead, we asked for loyalty, for service. No money could initiate the ties of blood which were proposed. Only loyalty.

When the stars woke the next summer, we knew it was time to gather the men as wolves.We walked through the valley, and they descended at the sight of us—— first seven, and then seventy times seven. We raided all around us who were foolishly heavy, and our own horses grew fat on the forage all summer. As our herds increased it came time for the Gathering.

We were twenty-seven years old on the day of the Gathering. In the morning, Temujin was the picture of health, of masculine vitality, of pride. As the sun lowered itself before him, however, the fits came, and he gasped for breath. The Wise One came to call down spirits upon him, and to exile others. Our wolves could not see him this way.

At nightfall, the Khan-to-be walked before the host and was declared leader in splendid garb: in gold, in silk, and in fine wool felt. A belt of ivory plaques and a tall cap distinguished the Khan from the masses. Braided horns cascaded over masses of fur. Great shouts of joy and of hope came from the strongmen gathered around us. A banner was raised: the emblem, a female hunting falcon. Fires burned taller that night.

After over a decade of strength in alliance, our relationship with the Kereyids turned bitter. War came. We could not retreat to Mount Burkhan Khaldun to renew our strength, but were pushed to the east, to the land of our mother's people.

Our herds dwindled from disease, and our army was starving. At every turn Temujin and I were reminded of the sting of the plow. My palms would sweat always, and Temujin's neck remembered its old position, craning forward at a pained angle. I do not know if the attacks on his breath——which had ceased in our prime——had returned because we were so hungry, or because our horses were worn thin with disease, or because of his war with his former blood-brother. He asked constantly for water, more water. He would wade out into the shallows of the lake even on the windiest days.

But on the last day of high summer he fell into convulsions, and died.

His nokor helped me to wrap his body in fine garb. He had told us what to do before he died, but we were appalled, and only from fear of his spirit did we obey. We gathered stones and tied them to his shroud. The Great Khan's body sank into the deep, and was never to be seen again. I watched its descent for as long as I could, knowing that my hands were wrapped in all that fine cloth, that my hands gripped his jade disc and gold hunting knife. Temujin's true hands hung uselessly at my sides.

From that time on, I wore my brother's clothes and I slept in his tent. Borte, his wife, kept quiet the secret. It could not be known that Temujin had succumbed at last to the breath-thief, and that his bones were sunk in the deep. It took me most of an evening to wipe all the yellow makeup away from my forehead, and to shave off much of my hair, which was heavy with animal fat. As a child, I had learned to plait Temujin's hair, and now I set to the task on my own head, carefully forming the braids above my ears so that they cascaded over my shoulders as masculine horns. Our clothes and our weaponry had always been the same, but I was careful to pad my shoulders with extra scarves, hidden beneath my deel. We spread the story abroad that his twin sister had died, and all were quick to believe it. Death comes so easily to those who are not careful.

After weeks of distress, the white camel appeared. It stood upon the horizon like a mirage. Autumn had dried the soil and pushed forward grapes from the vines, so distant from us there, by the lake. Its high steps were majestic, and the clothes of its leader,

Hassan, seemed to blur at the edges. He brought us food from his caravan in exchange for protection on his way. Never had I heard of such a thing. I think he found us pitiful, after witnessing the power of the Kereyids to the west. We attended him for two months and found our strength restored.

Those lean times had turned our spirits to spit and vinegar. No longer wanting in our bodies, we found ourselves hungry all the same, haunted by the feeling of lack. No matter how much we ate, our flesh cried out. The insults of our enemies hung in the air around us like so many flies. I led our armies in raids once again, and this time our ferocity was unquestioned. Men defected from all directions to join us and take part in the fire.

Fear had been slaked from our dreams. The Father above and Mother below found union in our campaigns, and we were greatly blessed. Inspiration came as the rain, desires for greatness swirling in our whispers. The desires were declared sanctioned by the wise and sustained by the wishes of the steppe.

The world was under the trampling hooves of our horses at last.

"I am brought low, baatar," she said to Bilgeh, "and my story cannot go on longer tonight. Pain runs down my limbs, and my memories grow dim with the nightfall. I tell you these things that my many angers may be diminished, and my people secured." A long pause broke her speech. He lifted his chin from his knee, where it had rested throughout her story.

"Do not mark my grave," she finally said, "whatever else you should do to my Empire, do not call the wretched upon the last bed of its lifeblood. I will not have my hunting knife wrenched from my bones."

The blood drained from Bilgeh's face. Having said her piece, she motioned with her hand that he should leave the tent. He exited backwards, eyes fixed upon her wrinkled face, until he reached the threshold, and stepped carefully over the tall wooden beam, fearing that he should knock it and incite her famous wrath. When the cold night wind embraced his shoulders and kissed his cheeks, it struck him that at long last he knew the truth.

His patron was the Shadow––the terror of cities, the spirit which animated the world's greatest empire––and the Shadow of the Great Khan was dying.

He went to find Altani.

WORM IN THE WOOD

By L.E. Smith

Prologue: In 1521, Martin Luther, then professor of theology at Wittenberg University, was summoned to the town of Worms to defend his public condemnation of the Catholic Church. As a result of the heat generated and of the perceived threat to the church, Luther was declared, after the debate, an outlaw justifiably executed by any righteous Catholic. Luther's abduction/murder was then staged by supporters to fool the church. He went into hiding as Junker (Sir) Jorge — gone from a monk to a knight. What follows is fictional, historical speculation on the extent to which Luther's friend Lucas Cranach (artist, Mayor of Wittenberg, apothecary, favored of the Court of Saxony) was involved in Luther's change of identity and protection. At the time of this story, Lucas Cranach is at home speaking to his wife Barbara, who will reveal her own concerns.

Lucas Cranach at the Fireplace (interior monologue)

"'Lord, serf, priest, publican! or what you are soever wrapped in blue swaddling, bless me as I bless you!' Here the asthmatic drew a breath and waved ordnance in our faces. 'But do you stop riders before I prick you with my pike!' That's what the watch said to us, Barbara, at the arch of west gate beneath Coswiger Tor hours before Van Amsdorf that pulled an empty dray cart. Empty! Ha! He cannot know Martin Luther rode beside me all wrapped and hooded in royal blue seated on a palfrey. And the watch does not seem to know me even now. Not thankful for the job I conferred upon him to ease him through his dotage, he with the young wife and a rogue's spite.

"You would think daybreak neglectful in penetrating his stony niche where the watch in greasy bear skin dozes as solemnly as cork in a bottle. Why, he stumbled and nearly impaled himself on his own halberd. We stopped at the gate in deference to custom. Can you just see, Barbara, his old muzzle snuffling the air to confirm the watery outlines of his sight. Ha! He is comedy on the boards, a morality play of sloth and pique. He is too much blemish upon us, as I have said to the Elector, Duke Frederick.

"And the watch has become increasingly proprietary in his moods, refusing immediate ingress to all but the Elector himself, as though each traveler has come to soil his pallet by rubbing thighs with his daughter, and she with the boils for itching. And he swats horses' rumps at egress, shouting even to pilgrims of our holy shrines. 'Begone, cutpurse!' and 'Speed away, pestilence!' What impression must we Saxons make upon travelers, whereupon Duke Frederick has replied to me: 'By comparison, we of the town will seem wonders of humility. Let him bark that we may seem to mew.'

"But I am tired to distraction that this man's shrewish wife has litigated me, Barbara, ME, mayor and second citizen after the Elector himself. Six times she litigates me, most lately for the death of her boy child that fell to the courtyard from its nest in the watchtower. Why can't she have roosted the boy better with that fat ass of hers? Why can't she be more like the lusty fish wives of the canal that I have passed at sunrise this day in the sleet and slipping in these Spanish boots that sometimes hobble me. I must have the tacking looked to. But even so they do eye me admiringly, Barbara. The wives. They lean away and eye me as they pull at oak-thatched cages immersed along the river banks that hold the perch, white arms bare even in this weather, and such a strong smell of fish, evocative also I suppose of decay — odd that Christ's sign should smell so musky of life and death together. And one of these may have a shape suitable for my painting of the Judgment of Paris, Barbara, as I infer by the calf of her leg jutting from her kirtle and the bodice swinging with such youthful flounce. I'll have her at the studio soon.

"And you should have heard Nicholas Van Amsdorf before the Elector, arrived hours late. I sat muffled in silence behind the Venetian screen, a hand pressing these bristles beneath my nose to prevent a leak of mirth, and much contained of myself. I can still smell fish, I swear, off these hairs even now. Van Amsdorf shook uncontrollably, thinking he had lost Martin Luther by abduction as their trundle in the forest of Waltershausen had been interrupted by violence. And why should he not think so? Martin had at the Diet of Worms insulted both Pope and the Emperor Charles in his debate with Aleander on indulgences.

"And did we indeed indulge! The pamphleteers had done their job to welcome the Papists — sarcastic poems in Virgilian ode tacked along the street greeted Aleander at Worms. And, I am told, he was bedded with his horse at stable — though no less a flea bite than the Inn that kept me I'll warrant. And at the debate, such a pout from that child Emperor to make us think he might fathom what was said! Ha! An ill-mannered boy whose portrait I have limned flatteringly in the relative quiet of 1508. Well, those were my early days.

"And in the forest, as I say, where I and several hirelings of the Duke lay waiting, Nicholas Van Amsdorf received a pummeling by my design, a mummery of Luther's abduction and final moments. It was enacted so beautifully. Then to think that Nicholas was bullied by the watch at the gate, as Nicholas complained — Ha! nothing new there — and Nicholas awakening Herr Duering the stabler before matins, surrendering up a winded horse and bloodied cart (chicken blood — he could not know) at the Staedtischer Marstall. Then Nicholas bade the mendicant monks of that order nearest the stables to open their doors early for prayer, keepers of the Antoniterkappelle, that small chapel with the delicate spires and an altar that shines like ivory, one of your favorites, Barbara.

"Well, and so he said to the Duke, 'We who have seventeen thousand holy relics enshrined in the Castle Church now look to our Elector, Frederick the Wise, he said in a deep breath as if baited in the hunt, as indeed he was, he said further,' we look to your grace to provide the bones of our most recent martyr, Martin Luther, declared volgelfrei by the Roman Curia, so that he may be executed by any vengeful Christian with impunity, though no good Saxon would lay on and did not certainly, though someone did. Not, perhaps so sacred, his bones, as the thorn of Christ or vial of milk from the Virgin Mary (Nicholas signed the cross at this moment — high theatrics), but they will ensure Wittenberg's place in Pilgrimage. We must have Luther's bones!'

"Oh, what tripe! And of course, the Duke knowing Luther will this night sit before my easel a new man — Junker Jorge, sir knight in hiding. He will soon be writing treatises from the castled walls of sanctuary. I will paint his tonsuring pasted in with horse hair, of which my apprentice workshop will copy many times this secular icon that will, perhaps, outsell his monkish visage. Sell him as martyr! Nonsense! Sell him resurrected reformer! His God made flesh will route the Romish and unite our principalities. Some just don't know the marketplace. And of course Nicholas Van Amsdorf looks to reclaim his prominence at University with Luther gone, this Nicholas that long ago, and before Luther's fiery arrival at Wittenberg, had led the Scotist's debate against the Thomist faculty. It was a dialectic wrangle made famous in the north by pamphleteers. Ha! These firebrands know their job! Nicholas, at that time, had audience with whosoever he pleased, as he had won the debate by exposing (and this was low!) Aristotle for a fool — he the father of St. Thomas's thinking. Amsdorf said the old philosopher had, enamored of Alexander's wife Phyllis, been found in the garden with a saddle on his back and a bit in his mouth carrying the queen on all fours to prove to her his love. Alexander, said Amsdorf, looked on from behind the plant fronds. But who has not been humbled by a woman? Am I not right, Barbara? Have we not played the sport of horses in our own fashion ... Ha!

"And poor Nicholas shook in his bones before our Duke the Elector, who could not help notice the corrupt tincture of his skin, the greasy flax of his hair. And it did not help that the watch at the gate had shaken his lance with surly indifference at Nicholas' academic gown. And as sleet stung his face while he leaned exposed into the wind and foul breath of that broken-toothed soldier, all the more bullying for having been made to leave his fire, Nicholas must have despaired of ever receiving warmth again, from either mankind or the elements, after his failed mission as Luther's guardian. Oh, that's rich!"

* * * * *

Barbara Cranach (interior monologue)

Seventeen years my husband and still robust and meaty enough for a wise old cook like me. And that beak nose severe as Punch that tickles me snuffling along the thigh beneath my night clothes. Did Lucas say the watch snuffles? Not so much as he. Even now he kicks the footstool playfully aside which must disturb the worms at their meal of ottoman oak and send them into excelsior to escape the thunderings of that indifferent boot. But to me a broad wink and a galliard look at his well-shaped leg in hose — no bombast stuffed round the shank for this manly man that has come from God complete.

And he must be motion as he speaks, and so rounds me as I sit; his gnarly hand comes down my neck unto my bodice — "Tis only fustian," he would say of late and roll the fabric from my bosom till it strains near tearing. But he has seen the tailor's bill of buckram and of the pinking done to window the cambric linen underneath, and so he only pets me to the nipple where he pinches then retreats, but talks of some fish wife's fig upon his lip that's been his morning pleasure as he intimates. Have her "at the studio"! Aye and a time or two before.

He is gone to tease the salon fire unto heat. And though I poke him in the thigh with my embroidery needle, directly where God's angel dislocated Jacob's interior hip, he does not tell me I have the sting of an angel, as he does so often at our impious times. And I know by the blue veins pulsing at the interstices of his narrowing eyes that Lucas has touched me, not as man does woman, but as lightning does the Salniter. I am, for a moment, the "prima materia" of his alchemical stumblings toward self-knowing. But this is too lofty. I am more like the fire sparking onto the rush mat that he crushes meanly with his Spanish boot, the wormwood that is strewn onto the floor to discourage fleas, the herbs to balance off the spaniel's urination. I am just here, always, a bother or a service. And I am flush with a notion of the day so strong that I would just as lief have it sleep awhile beside the fire.

But he must politic me unto worry. What care I that Martin Luther will feign death to hide from an angry Pope and boy-child Emperor. What care I that Wittenberg's Duke Frederick supports a misanthrope as town watch. And the shrew that litigates will have judgment when she's called to a higher court. She is no more than a fig passed over at the marketplace. And Van Amsdorf ... that officious fool, gets what he deserves. Even as he is duped as Martin Luther's failed bodyguard.

Yes, and once again Lucas must have Phyllis ride the back of Aristotle. Why can this story mean so much to him? Unless this be the analogue to improper behavior, his judgment of Alexander's wife. Does he want me so watered down that I must weep at the sight of gardens? A quiet woman with cats? Is he disturbed that I suggest a naked likeness in paint of Katharina Von Bora for the trunk lid of Martin Luther's secular life in exile? For him to dream on. And Katharina, that I must rescue from her gray cell of the convent. Let her break the vows! That she can't touch a man but Jesus ... that she can't touch herself ... that I can put all her life till now in sampler epigrams upon this embroidered pillow draws me to sadness. I'll murder the cats and poison the garden before I'll let her rot another year in moral excess! She must perforce be Luther's wife.

Well and I am perhaps too much a wife. I must seem to be one of those matrons painted by the Dutch, as I have no life outside this framed interior. While on his present canvas, that I peek at wandering sleepless with a candle, Lucas does not dare circumscribe and confine the three naked graces that Paris must choose among. Their woodland runs all the way to distant mountains. They gambol upon the horizon as I tinker this side of a coffered window. And these are ladies of the court of Saxony, I notice, that come to the back door of the studio to strip away their clothes. But why are they so bored in likeness in the paint? Perhaps this is the truest mood of ladies waiting to be chosen. Or perhaps they know the lovely Anna who has become a favorite of my husband in his studio. And when looked hard at, in this scene of three, Anna seems to be all of one and verily all the body parts. If Paris must have his judgment, let this be it: They call her love-worn Anna, as in her name they see her heels come over her head so easily.

OPUS ONE

By Amadea Tanner

The Dempsey Quintet pulsed eight to the bar, breathing life into the madcap melee. Walter Dempsey, center stage, had the crowd crazed for more, singin' 'bout rhythm itself so every soul on the floor could be swept up in the metaphor of the moment.

This was The Place, as hoppin' as it was happening, where dancing was non-negotiable, and stamina sacrosanct. From the way patrons talked about it, you might think it was for the best of the best, and it was, but "best" had a new meaning on those spring-loaded floorboards. No one who was anyone in the real world would have dared step over the threshold, not if they knew where life was taking them. The Place was for the stranded, the dreamers, the transitory, where lost souls could find direction in their soles; all the working-class girls with their one night off and the boys who couldn't cut the draft. All together they were a heap of hepcats hyped on their good fortune, fortune savored particularly because under any other circumstances it would be anything but.

So they danced all night, because they were free to do so.

Because it was all they could do.

The band took a brassy breath with the end of the song and then took it slow into the next. The trumpeter stepped forward, filling the room with a sound that was soft and forlorn until the drums tapped out a swift rhythm in answer. It was the tempo of a heartbeat aflutter, like so many beating just so on the dancefloor, bringing the floor alive with the sentimental sound of dreams.

But it was the dreams in one girl's eyes that gleamed beyond all others with the force of her longing for them to come true.

She sat coyly enough to suggest she'd like to dance but ignored the contents of the crowd. A band of soldiers had crashed the party an hour ago and the regulars didn't have the heart to throw them out. And the soldiers, well, they knew they didn't belong, but on the eve of being shipped overseas they didn't belong anywhere, really. Some of the gals didn't hesitate to wrap themselves in the arms of a man in uniform, but this gal preferred to keep her distance from posers in pomp and pomade.

One snuck into her periphery, however, and extended a hand with such presumption that no words accompanied the gesture. She met his gaze, challenging him to speak, so he said, "May I have this dance?"

"That mean I'm supposed to dance with you?"

"I'd like very much if you would."

"Fine," she sighed. "If you promise to remember me."

The soldier wanted to say he couldn't possibly forget her, that his memory had become as sharp as if he was seeing his life flash before his eyes, because he knew this was all he would have. He knew she knew that too, but she probably heard that from every man in his monkey clothes who asked her to dance. She must be getting awful tired of the melodrama.

She took his hand and looked past his shoulder as his other fumbled for her waist. They were quickly swallowed up with the tide of dancers, reminding the girl that if she wasn't remembered, she could very easily fade into the worn fabric of the world, a single stitch irrelevant for wont of a bigger picture.

The boy murmured with rehearsed precision, "What's your name, Darlin'?"

"That'll do just fine."

"I can't remember you like that. What do they call you 'round here?"

"Truce. Short for Chartreuse, but let's just skip the formalities."

But he grinned, beseeched. "Where'd you get a name like that?"

"That's the trouble, isn't it?" she muttered. "With a name like mine, that's all anyone ever wants to talk about. I'm getting awfully tired of sharing my origin story in the span of a song."

The real trouble was that the extent of her story could fit into the span of a song. Chartreuse Evans was told her name came from a mother who was eccentrically French, and who shortened the darned thing to "Truce" because it seemed like a fine thing to come between a man and a woman in a perpetual state of war. But that wasn't enough to stop the fighting, and when good ol' Pops went off for good and died in the real war, somewhere in a French foxhole, Truce's mother found this to be a sort of poetic justice. As a peacetime peace offering, she handed young Truce off to her in-laws and returned to La République, leaving Truce to grow up in a small town in a big world, where she developed the hint of a drawl and the gradual realization that life was a series of questions without answers, a state of being that cultivated within her a desperate obsession to uncover something greater. And that brought her life up to the present moment, in the arms of another clammy soldier boy, at another Friday night send-off dance in the midst of another war.

"You from around here?" the boy asked, to prove he was an ardent conversationalist in lieu of his lack of rhythm. Truce finally looked him in the eyes, and he was frozen in place, because her gaze was not the kind you could look away from.

"I wish I could say I was just passing through. Because life's a journey, right? At least I've always dreamed that's what it's supposed to be."

The boy looked at her strangely, a glimmer of recognition surfacing to consciousness, but by the time the song ended, all he managed to say was, "You're good. You really know how to follow."

Her opinion of him flickered to flagrant neutrality. "That's because I let you lead."

"Let me lead one more?" He failed to hide his pride—of course he thought her words a compliment. But she had already abandoned him to melt into the tangle of cotton, brass buttons, and perfumed extremities that made up the surrounding crowd.

It was a well-worn understanding, she thought, that men led and women followed, that a follow was only as good as her lead, and that even with a bad lead, a good skirt with a grand swish could save them both. But what was less often acknowledged was the wizened telepathy that came with being flung across a dancefloor by every so-called man in town. There were only so many moves in the stockpile; after dancing long enough, a follow could recognize what a lead planned to cue even before he'd thought it through himself. One might interpret that the follows were the ones actually leading; they just couldn't take the blame or claim the glory for themselves.

Truce could lead or follow as good as any. From afar, she was indistinguishable from the rising tide of feminine wiles—coiffed curls, rouged lips and creaseless skirts. It was only when she turned and looked right at you that you couldn't look away. There was something in her eyes, something deep, dark, and strangely inviting. They were grey eyes, cold, but forgiving, glistening with a look halfway between lost and lonesome, a look she only ever used to get when caught up in a crowd.

Now this look was with her all the time, perhaps because Truce now spent every night dancing. It was the easiest way to get away when you had nowhere to go.

But a gal could only escape into a song so many times. She blamed her bitterness on the new boys passing through town who didn't know a thing about left from right, or right from wrong. It was so easy to blame anyone—anything—everyone —everything. That was what they all did because there was something dark and ominous forcing them to wait, for big things like peace and even little things like love. It was the waiting, perhaps, that left Truce feeling starved and unlucky. She had waited all her life to grow up so that she might start living as a woman in the world, only to ripen in time for life to go stale as the whole world cowered in the shadow of the moon.

Truce wandered over to the bar in the corner, where Karen Braddock was sliding the GIs Gin Rickeys across the counter. Karen was a pleasant barmaid to the regulars, but tonight with soldiers crowding round, she was treating the gig with the somber decorum of a real Charon, ferrying lost souls a little nearer to their doom. Granted, the way the boys were drinking, they were doing a pretty good job of ferrying themselves.

They drank and cavorted with equal abandon, their laughs the bright peals of immortality since enlisting meant they were guaranteed heroes. It made nobodies into somebodies. It gave them all a living legacy with a cause to die for.

More importantly, it gave them a purpose. And though these boys were off to seek an untimely demise, Truce envied them, because they had tapped the wellspring of greater meaning, even if it was only temporary. Because if they died, they died for a reason. These drunken fools had a reason, and it had been handed right to them.

Meanwhile, Truce was stuck on the sidelines. Maybe that made her lucky. Why, then, did it make her feel sick? She could no longer tell if she was green with envy or remorse.

"You really ought to stop looking melancholic in public places, Trucie," Karen interrupted. "It's not good for your image."

Truce smiled half-heartedly in response.

"What are you drinking?" Karen asked.

"Anything," Truce muttered. "I need a major slake."

Karen smirked as she began to mix some kind of elixir. "The boys have been talking about you. I'd be jealous if I didn't already recognize the curse of celebrity."

"If the boys had a care," Truce shot a glance towards the men in uniform at the other end of the bar, "they could do me the honor of dancing in time."

Karen nodded. "Amen."

"How's Harvey?" Truce asked.

"Oh, you know. Wants to propose, but I told him there's no point getting married if he won't be coming back."

"Above collecting a widow's pension?"

"It's not that, it's the darn principle of the thing. If he wants to make a vow, it sure as hell better be one he can keep." Karen sighed, "Till death do us part sounds a bit foreboding anyway, don't you think?"

"Glad to see you've come to your senses."

"I don't think I have. It's just that war's gone and stripped all the romantic notions I had to spare. Sometimes I wonder if rationing has done a number on my emotional capacity; I've become a real pragmatist."

Truce smiled a real smile at that. "Funny thing, isn't it? They've all turned into saps and we've become heartless."

"I think all this sentimental swing is a government ploy."

"To keep up morale." Truce agreed.

"And keep our poor troops running on the sheer pangs of heartache. It's sickening. That's why they don't even bother asking us to dance, isn't it? We're just a guarantee. Five minutes with a pretty girl 'cause they might not ever see one again. Does that make them fools or heroes?"

"A bit of both, I should think," Truce sighed, accepting the cocktail Karen slid across the bar top. She pursed her lips after a tentative sip, then gulped the whole thing down.

"Anyone operating with good sense never gets remembered."

She made the mistake of glancing once more towards the soldiers, where one of them had been waiting to meet her gaze. He took her eyes as an invitation to step forward and inched closer with the looks of a long list of ticklish questions on the tip of his tongue, the first of which he murmured lamely:

"Would you like to dance?"

How polite of him to ask, she thought, but what a funny question that was. Truce was more accustomed to "May I?" and "Shall we?" which were inquiries that implied an answer in the affirmative. Perhaps it was simply redundant to ask a gal at a dancehall if she would like to dance; Truce realized she preferred the presumption. It kept her from asking things of herself. Did she want to dance? Did she really?

She nodded instinctively because that's what she always did. But as the soldier led her to the edge of the dancefloor, Truce realized she didn't really wish to dance at all. She'd danced too much for too long, every night for as long as she could remember. It used to feel good, it used to make her smile. But now, Truce realized her soles had begun to ache something fierce.

All through their twisting and swaying to the music, she could only think of how much she didn't really want to dance with this soldier, which got her thinking about all the soldiers she'd been with since the open call to enlist. She hadn't wanted to dance with most of them, but she had forced herself to laugh when they'd tried cracking jokes, and she had been a good sport about kissing the ones who claimed they'd never been kissed. At least she never intended to make good on any of the hasty proposals she'd accepted just to make their askers feel important before they crossed an ocean. She hadn't wanted to do any of it, but guilt, pity, civic duty made her do it.

No, those were just excuses. Even if she hadn't wanted to do any of those things, she had done them anyway, because she didn't know what she wanted.

Swallowing up someone else's passion, hearing about someone else's dreams at least got her thinking that she could do something too. And she knew she could do it, if only she knew what that something was. But in a town where nothing happened, in a life where, even on the dancefloor, she had only ever followed someone else's lead, she didn't know what else there was to do. This was a town where people waited for life to happen to them, then grew old with waiting and finally got around to little things so they could at least say they had done something for themselves. Dancing had been a good way to pass the time, but now enough had passed that Truce was starting to feel time itself pass her by.

The trick, she supposed, though had never achieved, was contenting oneself with dreams that could be attained. The gals around here were only working to wait for their boys to come back so that they might fulfill their dreams of a family. And those boys were off dying for ideals in hopes of coming home to a job—any job—so that they might be the man of a house. There was nothing the matter with dreaming dreams such as those, and Truce suddenly admired everyone else immensely for having the courage to seek contentment. Maybe she envied them a little too, for knowing what they wanted. All she knew for herself was that nothing was ever quite enough.

And people everywhere all the time said it was wrong to want more, but wasn't that what everyone was fighting for, in this war and every one before it? Well, she was sick of people, sick of these people. She wanted to meet new ones in new places with new grand ideas. This would have been an easy feat, considering she had been stranded in the same town for the entirety of her life. But now, all over the country, suddenly everywhere was the same, everyone doing the same things, thinking the same ideas, rallying to the same cry. Perhaps that was why her eyes shone the way they did; lost, lonesome, finding only contempt in the crowd's contentment.

Truce only wanted, somehow, to be remembered like all these boys whose names would be etched into history. Thinking about all the numbers going into this fight was enough to make anyone feel small. But knowing that she would never be included among those ranks, it might as well be as though she'd never existed. What was it all for then, if you wouldn't be remembered?

As Truce was dancing with the latest soldier, the Dempsey Quintet struck up an especially merry tune. But it was eerie to have such light-hearted notes pierce through the heaviness in the air. It always amazed Truce, how a sound could be something a body could feel. Beyond rhythm, beyond emotion, some melodies could reach so deeply they seemed to stir the soul. Truce wondered if that was why everyone had souls in their feet too.

Sick of being pensive, she looked up at her dance partner and asked to be polite, "What's your name, Soldier?"

"Johnny." He smiled. "And yours?"

"Chartreuse."

His smiled broadened. "That so?"

"Don't you forget it."

"How could I ever forget a name like that?"

She stared at him for a moment; there was that usual ironic, half-joking hint in his tone that they all spoke with. But half-joking meant half-serious. Truce thought about all the boys she'd been with swapping stories overseas about a gal back home called Chartreuse. She supposed it was a name to be remembered.

And that was something.

It was hardly anything, but it was better than nothing.

And though she was sick of it—all of it—Truce let this soldier hold her close, and let another one take over when a new song began. She danced with all of them, late into the night, just as she always did.

Because it was all she could do.

THE CAPUCHIN, THE CAT, AND THE PHILOSOPHER

By Salinda Tyson

Paris, 1720s

Philippe was the best waiter the café had ever had, and a favorite of Monsieur Voltaire. The fact that he was a monkey did not concern the writer and philosopher, who was a very pragmatic fellow, grateful that the beast could sniff out the king's censors, and howl to warn of their approach. When he was excited by ideas, the passionate scribbler's words flew off the paper, just as he lifted his pen, and escaped into the atmosphere of the café. There they floated before the eyes of wondering customers and regular patrons, who thus received a political education and thought more deeply than they might have otherwise. By clapping his hands, Voltaire could transform the air-borne calligraphy into ordinary pipe smoke, a handy talent if royalist agents visited the café.

Bright-eyed Philippe, who had previously belonged to a magician, hooted at the drifting words of philosophy, often swatting playfully at them. As a waiter, he could smoothly navigate and evade human legs and table legs, chitter and scurry across the floor and the tabletops, while carrying a steaming, perfectly balanced demitasse, his dark, hairy fingers hooked through the tiny handle, all without mishap, and deliver a steaming cup of coffee to the philosopher--who often partook of 40 such cups daily-- without spilling a drop.

His green uniform, tailored and sewn lovingly by Madame Robert, the café owner's wife, fit him perfectly and amused the neighborhood urchins. He wore a smart plumed hat fastened with ribbons to keep his fur from getting in coffee and pastries. His white mane framed his face like a judge's wig.

How Philippe had come to the café was a mystery shrouded in rumor. Gossips said Monsieur Robert had once, before his marriage, loved a young circus performer who owned Philippe, and that on her tragic death, Monsieur Robert had taken in the orphaned monkey. Of course, café patrons did not dare ask Madame Robert about this story. So ... Who knows? But Madame had no children, so the clever little beast had remained in the establishment, as valued worker, as constant amusement, and as beloved rascal. Besides, the little waiter did not need to receive tips or pay -- except for food, and fruits like bananas.

His favorite was oranges, which he could juggle, thanks to the magician's teaching.

Philippe delighted in stealing whatever café customers held in their hands. He would snatch an object, scamper away, and hold it in his tiny paws-- he especially liked just-lit pipes, on which he would puff solemnly, then cough. Smoke rings would dance in the air about his head, intertwining with Voltaire's witticisms. He would chatter and howl, screw his tiny face up, return the pipe to its owner, and bow.

An incurable mimic, he aped patrons to perfection, including Voltaire himself. The wit had a habit of pursing his lips as if suppressing a witticism at someone's expense, and his eyes sparkled with intelligence and mischief under a prominent brow ... His favorite color was green, and often he wore a green jacket with a flowing white cravat. So Philippe had a tiny green jacket.

Patrons enjoyed the spectacle of the café's cat--which rumor said had been a witch's familiar -- and the capuchin hissing at each other...

Oh, Philippe could become fierce, his lips pulled back over his teeth as he glared at the feline, Soupçon, or Suspicion, a big tom with smoke-colored fur and wild, demonic yellow eyes. Cat and capuchin had drawn up a mysterious truce between them, a silent, instinctive animal agreement. The cat stalked the floor. He chased any calligraphy that neared the floor, leaping on it and playing with it like a trapped mouse. The little monkey patrolled the bar, the tables and chairs, and the two ate in different spots -- sacred territory that neither invaded, on pain of bites and claw marks.

"If only human beings had the wisdom of these two," Voltaire said one day, watching keenly as the duo made their rounds. "But ... Common sense is not so common." His scrawled adage leaped into the smoky air, circled twice, and soared through an open window.

For all that Monsieur Voltaire was perpetually on high alert, he sometimes became so absorbed in his writing, in his thinking, that his surroundings blurred.

For those occasions, Philippe was invaluable. True, although he often lazed, snoozed, or groomed his pelt for fleas that he cracked between his teeth, any threat to the philosopher brought him instantly alert.

* * * * *

Monsieur Voltaire, born Francois-Marie Arouet, kept one eye cocked for the secret police, or those he suspected might be informers eager to ingratiate themselves with royalist agents. He had been tossed into the cells of the Bastille as a young man – for questioning and criticizing the church, society, and the monarchy. He took precautions, using false names when his poems and books were published. But even so, the public executioner often burned his tracts and books, for their mockery of the church, the royal regents, the Catholic religion in general, and the government in particular.

"Ah, Philippe," Voltaire said as the nimble capuchin set a cup and saucer before the notorious customer. "Merci, mon ami."

The writer petted Philippe on his doll-sized head, looked into his bright dark eyes, and bowed his head solemnly. "Bon matin, mon cher," the man of letters said. The capuchin touched his tiny cap and bowed in return. Voltaire tipped him generously with a small bag of nuts. The essayist stared into the depths of his demitasse as Philippe, clad in his smartly tailored miniature footman's uniform, hopped from table to bench and back to the bar to await the next order... and to crack and munch on the treasured nuts. And sometimes fling the shells at patrons.

Voltaire kept his nose in the air, constantly sniffing not only the delectable aroma of brewed coffee and pastries and soup, but the swirl of political intrigue surging through the streets and quarters of the French capital. Paris was a hotbed of ideas, resentments, schemes, revolutionary thoughts, and criticisms of the ruling Bourbons, and their excesses. Voltaire's nose for danger was sharp and his sense of timing had been honed by what was becoming a long career of dashing for distant provinces or foreign shores. Whenever one of his tracts was printed, he leaped into a swift, stripped down carriage and fled for the Swiss or Dutch border. When furor over his vitriolic opinions had cooled, he would return.

So he was perpetually nervous, ever perched on the edge of his chair, drumming his fingers, or casting sideways glances at everyone who entered the business. He was constantly on the lookout for an agent bearing a *lettre de cachet*, a document accusing him of crimes, which could thrust him into a dungeon in the Bastille again. His own father had had such a letter served on the young man simply because he wanted to marry an uneducated woman.

Coffee fueled Voltaire's nervousness and his brilliance.

Luck was with the philosopher.

Philippe spotted a certain tall stranger enter Chez Robert. The monkey howled a challenge, and skittered across the floor, tripping the man who came to grab Voltaire. The little beast screeched, bit the man's leg, and fled. He leaped onto the bar and tossed steaming coffee and grounds into the agent's face. Voltaire clapped his hands, banishing half of his floating written words into smoke. Despite this, two scrawled comments floated free: "Judge a man by his questions, not by his answers." Rippling alongside flowed: "No authority should be immune to challenge by reason."

Monsieur Robert pulled his wife into the back room.

"*Diable!*" the agent screamed, blinded. He cursed, mopping his face with his cravat, and pawed coffee from his eyes, hair, and neck. He spat out grounds. Face red, he blinked, looking for the animal.

Voltaire, keeping his wits about him, sprang up and flung his chair in the agent's way, tripping him again. The agent fell on his face. Soupçon had been curled up on the philosopher's lap. Resenting the disturbance, he sprang onto the agent's shoulder, snarled, and swiped the man's face with a smoky paw. Cat and capuchin caught the ends of the still wafting slogans, pulled them tight as ribbons, and tripped the agent, who fell flat on his face. The string of incriminating words vanished under the cat's claws.

The *philosophe* ducked out a side door, which led to the theater district.

Philippe sat on a shelf, studying the chaos, clapping his hands and hooting. The agent stumbled up and plunged after the capuchin, who raced across tabletops and leaped atop the china cupboard. Every customer fled.

"*Mon Dieu! Diable!*" the man roared. He flung the gray tom across the room. Soupçon twisted in mid-air, landed on all four paws, crouched and snarled, ears laid flat against his head.

Monsieur Robert fetched a bucket of cool water for the agent.

"Keep those beasts away from me," the agent roared. He dunked his head face-first.

Voltaire, unable to resist watching the drama, peeked around the door of the café.

"Bon Dieu," he thought, "who probably doesn't exist, I thank whatever spirit created such loyal, magical animals!"

Smiling his crooked smile, he raced into the labyrinth of the old theater district, through a maze of alleyways, which he knew well – for many of his mistresses worked on the stage. Perhaps this time he would flee to England. Like bees, little words -- liberty and reason -- swarmed above his head before darting off to land on the rooftops of Paris.

From the café's back room, Madame Robert beckoned to Philippe.

She held up an orange.

"Viens, toi," she called to Soupçon and set out a dish of cream.

POETRY

Lynn Aprill

Joel Brickell

J. Thomas Brown

Wendy Howe

Billie Holladay Skelley

SESTINA FOR DOOLOUGH

By Lynn Aprill

"How can men feel themselves honoured by the humiliation of their fellow beings?"
Mahatma Gandhi

It was the fourth year of the Great Hunger--
four years of failed crops, nothing in fall
to put away against winter's bitter passage,
silent door frames filled with emaciated children.
Instead, Irish grain filled the bellies of English ships, crossed
the rolling Irish Sea, crammed English landlord mouths.

As Irish grain filled English landlord mouths,
the living skeletons of Louisburgh, the hungry
and destitute souls numbering six hundred, shuffled across
the frozen March ground, praying for relief to fall
from the coffers of union officials, leading their children
to be counted. Instead, they found an impasse-

no solace would be spared unless they passed
the night walking ten, fourteen, twenty miles to Delphi. Their mouths
agape at the injustice, they had no choice but to shepherd their children
through mountain passes and rubbled roads, their hunger
finding little comfort in grass and water mint. They fell
to their task, a frigid midnight journey, a bitter bridge to cross.

Through the night, the company stumbled across
the final miles, arriving at Delphi Lodge just past
daybreak. Their cries for relief and respite fell
on deaf ears, for the union men were filling their mouths
and would not be disturbed. The corpsed mothers, hungry
and weeping, gathered their wasted children.

The famished fathers cradled their dying children
and turned, intending to retrace bitter steps across
the valley, back to abandoned homes. But Hunger
had other plans, as one by one they passed
beyond the shores of the black lake, their mouths,
bellies, souls empty and, one by one, they fell.

Across the Great Water, the cries of Doolough fell
on the ears of the Choctaw children
who knew only too well the pain of empty mouths
and empty homes. As the help they had to offer crossed
the ocean, they prayed for the Irish Famine to pass,
for they, too, knew this shared hunger:

"Emptiness filling their mouths, they died where they fell,
their faces etched with hunger, clasping their silent children--
only a stone cross to mark their passing."

JS BACH
ADDRESSES THE FUGUE

By Joel Brickell

Doddering fugue in a gray key,
I have come for you.
Born in the time of the frowning masters,
Your clothes stretched too tight
On your ponderous frame –
They shackled you with rules, Fugue,
These men for whom laws and limits
Are outward and visible signs of God's love.
But I know God can dance.
And I will strip you naked, Fugue,
And I will twist and clothe you
In a thousand wild fashions.
You will teach God how to whirl,
How to prance, how to laugh.
Yes, we will start with their rules, Fugue,
But when our blasphemies are done
Our heresies will be their hymnal,
Our God, theirs.

GABRIEL
By J. Thomas Brown

Gabriel was a blacksmith who read of Haitian revolt,
how Toussaint Louverture defeated white Europeans
and threw off the shackles and yoke
On the Isle of Saint-Domingue, gone were pin and loop

In his mind he must have been baffled
by the words Thomas Jefferson wrote:
that all men are created equal,
yet he was counted but three fifths of a man

In Gabriel's vision of enlightened revolution,
if someone posed an impediment to freedom,
they would be put to death. Only
Frenchmen and Quakers could be spared.
But he never foresaw the matter of floods,
betrayal, and a pardon two centuries late

Betrayers told how his anvil rang like a church bell
as he beat the iron with his hammer,
forging pikes into spears, sickles into swords,
how he wore out bullet molds

He was tried by a court of five planters
whose arrogant hearts filled with fear
When they saw how well slaves plotted
they knew they had underestimated the man

Gabriel gave no names and accepted the blame
but told of his careful plan:
capture the armory, take hostage Monroe,
to deliver from bondage his sisters and brothers
and spread rebellion through the land

He rode on the tumbrel alone,
hands bound behind his back,
a West Coast African slave
steeped with the blood of Oonis
and no last name of his own

From the gallows in Shockoe Bottom
they hung him. Quietly standing
without a word, he accepted the noose,
then, soul let loose,
flew away on the wings of the wind.

TWO MARYS

By Wendy Howe

*A ghost said to haunt the castle, known as the "Pink Lady",
is thought to be that of the Queen.*

The Scotsman

I
(Stirling Castle, Scotland)

Do I move through stone walls? No
I glide within them -- a shaft
of gleaming satin. Sometimes you hear
my pink gown rustle, sometimes not.

But I have heard many
confuse my reign with hers -- *Bloody Mary*
first daughter of the heretic king.
Both queens, we shared the same name
and faith. Close to the breast, we held
a crucifix, our secret letters and sins, a lover's head,
my brave *James of Bothwell.*

Yet, the killings were hers. Pikes and swords
moved from field to town, stained
barn and tower scarlet. My hands were clean;
they clutched heather.

II

Do I breathe letting the tapestry flinch,
its lords and ladies lick dust? Perhaps,
but at one point, I also shared with her
the most grievous sigh -- the womb
befallen to an empty bowl. Hers

held the belief of a child
that stopped the menses, swelled the belly
until her condition waned
in truth. Nothing was there --
except the shadow of want.

Mine broke into sudden spasms
then blood. The twins' pulse
fell silent, their presence left
as pale moths to gnaw
holes in my voice. And I sobbed
killing the light.

Ozark Spite Dolls

By Billie Holladay Skelley

Long ago in the shadowy and bewitching forests of the Ozarks, they say
the devil was often glimpsed on a winding road or snaking pathway.
So frequent were his sightings in southern Missouri's hills and valleys,
settlers named the places where he was believed to routinely dally.
There was the Devil's Promenade, near Joplin, and the Devil's Kitchen Trail,
and folks could walk the Devil's Backbone to visit the Devil's Well.
In these secluded sanctum, faith healers often ruled the day,
but in many hidden hamlets, medicine men and witch women held sway.
In such dark places, magic and faith swirled indistinguishably in the same smoke,
and Heaven and Hell walked together, like brothers, coupled in a shared yoke.
Many lost souls felt they needed measures of protection each and every day,
just to keep demonic spirits and dangerous adversaries away.
Thus, they carefully crafted spite dolls of straw, beeswax, and wood,
and named them for their evil enemies who were up to no good.
Adorning them with pieces of burlap or bits of cloth to resemble a foe,
they took extra effort when the doll represented a fickle or wayward beau.
They punctured and stabbed these figures to inflict injury and pain,
so that their enemies might experience exactly the same.
By plunging a doll's feet into the fire three times or more,
they could keep an opponent from walking to their door.
Cutting a doll's limb could induce a rival's bone to break,
and a sharp blow to its brow might add a painful headache.
A hot needle to a doll's eye could produce blindness in a spy,
while a cold nail to its heart could cause a tormentor to die.
Using innocent dolls in such an odd way might seem quite strange today,
but who are we to say...
for frontier Ozark settlers facing a harsh and isolated life,
filled with dangers, treachery, and an abundance of strife,
from living where the devil dared to dance even in the light of day,
that spite dolls were not the best remedy for keeping evil away?

Writing Hotel Portofino

By J.P. O'Connell

The story of an English family who moves to Italy to open a guesthouse, *Hotel Portofino* is set in the titular coastal town in 1926. People ask me: did I go there to research it? Sadly not. (Blame COVID - I do.) But there's a lot you can find online nowadays - more maps and photos than any sane person could want - and there's more you can read in places like London's British Library, where I called up long-forgotten memoirs of Anglo-Italian life like Cecil Roberts' Portal to Paradise (sample quote: 'It has been said that Englishmen are born with two ineradicable loves - one for the England that breeds them, the other for the Italy that lures them') and wincingly hilarious travel guides from the period. Without fail these depict Italians as noble yet easily corruptible simpletons who have nevertheless managed, more by accident than design, to produce some of the world's finest art, literature, and cuisine.

The interwar period, when wealthy Westerners discovered the pleasures of 'abroad', is remembered (or misremembered, depending on your viewpoint) as the Golden Age of Travel. Taking advantage of the latest technologies - planes, trains, and automobiles - they crisscrossed Europe in search of exclusive hotels and ravishing beauty spots. If you had the time and the money, you could go skiing in St Moritz and then take the Blue Train from Paris down to the Côte d'Azur. From there you could drive along the coast to Monte Carlo for a spot of blackjack before crossing the border into la bella Italia...

Italy was one of the most popular interwar destinations. The barrier island in the Venetian Lagoon known as the Venice Lido became a magnet for the fashion-conscious super-rich. But the Italian Riviera, a crescent-shaped strip of rugged Ligurian coastline studded with pastel-coloured towns, appealed to the prosperous middle classes who valued its quaintness, its beauty, and the restorative comforts of its warm yet fresh climate.

Ever since the seventeenth century wealthy Brits had been stopping off in Italy on their Grand Tours. (Americans, too - see Mark Twain's bestselling travel memoir *The Innocents Abroad*.) For this reason, there was something proprietorial about how comfortable they felt in the country and how readily they colonised certain Riviera towns, opening English libraries and 'British Shops' selling Gordon's gin and Huntley & Palmer biscuits.

Italy also had massive cultural snob value. The merest exposure to its wealth of paintings, frescoes and historic buildings was held to be improving - an attitude roundly mocked by EM Forster in *A Room With A View*, published in 1908 and filmed to acclaim by Merchant Ivory in 1985. (Who can forget Judi Dench as writer Eleanor Lavish? 'A smell! A true Florentine smell! Every city, let me teach you, has its own smell...')

Forster was fascinated by the 'Italian temperament' and the English responses to it. Although they're set some twenty years before Hotel Portofino, for research purposes I reread both *A Room With A View* and the earlier *Where Angels Fear to Tread*, about a free-spirited English woman, Lilia, who defies her family by marrying the handsome young Italian man she met on holiday and remaining in Italy.

The free spirit in Hotel Portofino is matriarch Bella. The daughter of a wealthy industrialist, she's the driving force behind the hotel and channels her entrepreneurial zeal into forging a new life in Italy for her family. Her husband, Cecil, is an aristocrat (and a cad to boot) but like many of his kind in the 1920s he has no money. Which puts all the pressure on her.

Their artist son Lucian was badly injured in the trenches. He spent his convalescence reading travel guides to remind himself that a better life might one day be possible. Because this was no longer a prospect anyone took for granted. 'I do feel that during the war something in [England] got killed,' wrote Forster on his return home from India in 1922. Many other writers and artists felt the same way, fleeing to Mediterranean countries whose beauty and climate seemed to stand for the opposite of combat. The title of the WW1 memoir Robert Graves wrote after moving to Majorca - *Good-Bye to All That* - says it all, really.

For a historical novelist, reading novels from the period is the best research you can do, because above all you want your characters to feel real - and novels capture consciousness with a precision no other form can match. Elizabeth Bowen's 1927 debut novel *The Hotel*, based on a holiday the Anglo-Irish writer took not far from Portofino, was incredibly helpful in this respect; also in more obvious ways to do with how things looked, what people wore, and what the plumbing was like.

Just as useful, though, was a sequence of novels not published until the 1990s - Elizabeth Jane Howard's bestselling *Cazalet Chronicles*, which follow the fortunes of a well-heeled English family from just before WW2 until the 1950s. Like *Hotel Portofino*, the Cazalet books are as much character- as plot-driven. Their use of viewpoint is very revealing, both about the gestalt of family life and the way the most compelling drama often derives from the natural friction between characters rather than the violent contortions of plot.

So no, as it transpired I didn't need to go to Italy to research *Hotel Portofino*. But in a COVID-free world would I have wanted to?

Do you really need to ask?

www.ingramcontent.com/pod-product-compliance
Lightning Source LLC
Chambersburg PA
CBHW081104300726
48976CB00011B/2719